Dirt Trail Drifter

JACK REASON

A Black Horse Western

ROBERT HALE · LONDON

© Jack Reason 2000
First published in Great Britain 2000

ISBN 0 7090 6804 2

Robert Hale Limited
Clerkenwell House
Clerkenwell Green
London EC1R 0HT

The right of Jack Reason
to be identified as author of this work has been
asserted by him in accordance with the Copyright,
Designs and Patents Act 1988.

This for C and M
and the years they have yet to share

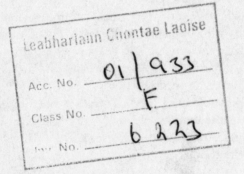
Typeset by
Derek Doyle & Associates, Liverpool.
Printed and bound in Great Britain by
Antony Rowe Limited, Wiltshire

One

It was an hour after first light on a morning in late Fall, with the frost as crisp as gravel and the sun already a blood-red ball, when they dragged Joe Blossom from his bed and rode him clear of Wargrit to his execution somewhere back of the San Apee dirt trail.

There were four in the party taking Joe to his death:

Marcus Pitch, one-time big name gambling man from back East who had sought his final refuge from mounting debt in the quiet of Wargrit for no better reason than he had happened there on the hope of his last dollar – and played a winning hand.

Cornelius Tove, another refugee, who had made his money fleecing the drunks and exploiting lost whores through Wichita, Amarillo and El Paso before investing the 'whole darned pile' in Wargrit's run-down Best Bet Saloon.

Jonas Bantry, small-minded, small in stature store-keeper with an imagination fuelled by fantasy and insatiable appetite for elevation to 'mercantile tycoon', as yet unfulfilled.

And bringing up the rear on that frost-bright, thin-aired morning was the fellow they all knew and only ever referred to as Loafer. This sullen-eyed, brooding man had hit Wargrit along of Tove and had stood to him as the town's unofficial gunslinger ever since. It had been Loafer who had finally rid Wargrit of its 'mealy-mouthed, pesterin' ' Sheriff McLey in a rigged gunfight on Christmas Eve twelve months back.

McLey had been buried rough, his badge of the law with him.

Four men silent, thoughtful, muffled tight against the sting of early cold, seated easy on their snorting mounts, passed like soft blurs through their misted breath; four men, each of them to their own cut, save for the look in their eyes, the bland glaze of resolve to a deed that would be done and their backs turned on it before the morning frost had melted. . . .

'Hell, fellas, yuh got this all wrong. Yuh ain't thinkin' straight. Yuh hear? Yuh just ain't thought it through.'

Joe Blossom, middle-aged, widowed years back, with little in the way of kith and nothing of kin, squirmed in the saddle of his droop-necked mount, his roped hands writhing against the bite of the bonds, the sweat, in spite of the frosted air, gleaming proud and beaded on his brow, his voice creaking and croaking like cracking ice.

'Yuh listenin' up there, f'Cris'sake?' he moaned, gaze flitting and flickering, wet and watery with fear, over the riders. 'Damnit, ain't none of yuh to carin'?' He squirmed again. 'Yuh'll hang for this, yuh know that, don't yuh? They'll string yuh up, every last one of yuh. I'm tellin' yuh. Ain't nobody gets away with this, not never. . . .'

But his words, it seemed, were already lost to the men leading him gently down the track. Perhaps they have heard them all before, or maybe they are of no count, anyhow, when the resolve is firm enough.

Joe grinned and began to titter. 'All some sorta joke, ain't it? This is all kiddin', puttin' the spooks in just for the hell of it, eh? I read yuh!'

Marcus Pitch granted a sidelong glance. Cornelius Tove sighed. Bantry looked a mite uncomfortable but stared doggedly ahead. Loafer hawked and spat violently.

'I know what yuh thinkin',' continued Joe, the sweat thickening, his breath swirling like a white veil. 'You're figurin' for me crackin', ain't yuh? You're reckonin' as how my nerve's gone on what I seen all that time back, night I just happened – just happened, mark yuh – to be walkin' off that sick gut I get on occasions. But, hell, that weren't nothin' to me, not one mite. What I seen had been comin' for weeks. We all knew that, McLey messin' with yuh like he did. Sure yuh had to get rid of him. Asked for it, didn't he? And Loafer there, well, he didn't fret none, did he? I'll say! Two shots, and that was it. McLey never so much as turned, never once showed his face. . . .'

Joe tittered again, but his flashing eyes mirrored his anxiety. The four men remained silent.

'All right, so mebbe I shouldn't have been there,

shouldn't have seen what I seen, but, hell, I ain't never said a word since, have I? Ain't never once breathed a sound, not to nobody, just kept yuh company, done like yuh've asked. . . . Yuh ain't got no cause to doubt old Joe Blossom, have yuh?'

Pitch cleared his throat and smiled softly to himself. Tove's glance was quick and coldly metallic. The storekeeper shifted uncomfortably. Loafer simply spat.

'Tell yuh somethin',' Joe blustered on, stifling a sudden shiver, 'if I had – *if* I had – blabbed so much as a word, half a word, come to it, why, I'd have taken that piece of mine and blown my head clean off, so I would. Would have, yuh can bet to it. But I ain't. Hand on my heart, I ain't. Believe me, don't yuh? 'Course yuh do. Heck we been partners for too long, ain't we? So let's cut this, shall we? Get ourselves back to town, somewhere warm. Mebbe crack a bottle, eh? What yuh say, fellas? We do that?'

Nobody answered; the stares stayed concentrated on the trail in the glow of the red-eye sun. Bantry pulled the collar of his coat tighter across his neck and wheezed softly on the thin morning chill. Tove blinked the icy dampness from his eyes. Marcus Pitch flexed his numbed fingers on the cold slip of rein leather. A thick pall of white breath swirled like a curtain from Loafer's mouth.

'Well, now,' huffed Joe, with an exaggerated shrug of his shoulders, 'that'll be the first time I known to any one of yuh passin' up the prospect of a bottle! What's with yuh? It too early? Yuh still sore-bellied from last night? Heads too thick?' He shuddered on the twitch of a struggling grin, narrowed his gaze, gathered his breath as if reaching a momentous decision. 'This got anythin' to do with that stage we got comin' in next month?' he croaked hurriedly. 'That what this is all about?'

Tove stiffened. Pitch rolled his eyes to the clear, high sky. Jonas Bantry shivered as he licked at a line of sweat on his lips. Loafer spat again.

'Right, aren't I?' Joe's eyes narrowed to dark, anxious slits. 'Too right I am! Well, so what? I ain't said as how I ain't for what yuh plannin'. I go along with it, sure I do. Thinkin's sound enough. All I said was as how I didn't want to see no killin'. Just that. No killin'. Won't be necessary, not if yuh do it proper – and I know yuh will, o'course. But if that's what's eatin' yuh, if yuh want for me to say as how I don't mind to a killin', sure I will. Yuh got it.' Joe spread a forced, anxious grin. 'That good enough? Can't say fairer, can I? If it comes to pullin' a piece on somebody and springin' lead, I'm with yuh. Hell, do it m'self if needs be!'

Cornelius Tove eased his mount to the right, away from the drift of the main trail to the frosted scrub and smooth-faced rocks circling the sprawl of an outcrop of boulders. Pitch followed, tightening his grip on the rope line to Joe's mount. Bantry buried his neck in his collar and swallowed on the cold emptiness in his stomach. Loafer's fingers spread like strands of a suddenly broken web over the butt of his Colt.

Joe Blossom's eyes widened again to fill his face like

round, wet moons. 'What's this?' he groaned, his voice scrambling deep in his throat. 'Where we goin'? What we doin' here, f'Cris'sake? This ain't no way to treat. . . .' The voice faltered, faded, barely audible now as Tove reined back to a halt, Bantry and Loafer flanking him, leaving Pitch to lead Joe and his mount to the dull morning shade of the tallest of the boulders.

'That'll do,' murmured Tove, when Joe was standing alone and separate from the four men facing him. 'Gunshot range in case yuh ain't noticed, Joe,' he added through a slow, dry drawl. 'Best way for it in the circumstances. We ain't for takin' chances.'

'No chances,' croaked Bantry hurriedly. 'That's right – no chances.'

'So we figure for this bein' fair,' added Pitch, spinning the chamber of a gleaming Colt. 'What yuh don't know and don't see ain't for botherin' us. What yuh harbourin', dies with yuh. Simple as that.'

'Now you listen up there,' began Joe, the sweat beading like ice on his face. 'Yuh'll hang, sure as hell yuh will. Yuh hear me? Yuh'll pay for this, long and hard. There'll be somebody, some time, from somewhere. . . . He'll be here, and yuh'll pay, every one of yuh. . . .'

'Too much talkin', Joe,' sighed Tove. 'That's the whole sum of yuh trouble – just too damned prone to too much talkin'.'

Four shots from four guns blazed across that frosted morning as if from one gun. Four aimed and measured shots that ripped deep into the chest and guts of Joe Blossom, throwing him back against the boulder in a floundering heap of arms and legs and a face full of eyes and gaping mouth where the sweat hung like icicles.

And when the body was finally still and its last twitch lost in the cloud of smoke and white misty breath, the four men eased silently out of the scrub, back to the trail that headed into Wargrit.

It was all done and over in no time at all.

TWO

Chance, and a swirl of buzzards circling high in the clear noon sky, had been at the root of the troubles that followed for John Kavanagh when he swung from the main trail out of San Apee to the dirt track heading west.

There was no good reason why he should have reined up when and where he did, save perhaps the drifting birds and the excuse to sate his thirst from his canteen; no good cause either for him to linger like he had, his pale-blue stare on the spreading wings, his thoughts content in the cool flow of creek water over his parched throat, but he had – and that, as he was to reflect later, had changed his life forever.

It was a whole long five minutes before Kavanagh stoppered the canteen, licked his lips, brushed a pestering fly from his cheek and came to watching the buzzards with a closer interest.

Two spurs to a pair of boots they were moving in for a feast, he thought, shading his eyes against the fierce glare; just waiting, he reckoned, for that moment when courage replaced curiosity and hunger got the better of hesitation, and they swooped, the big fellow there leading them in like a feathered downpour.

He grunted as his gaze shifted a mite to the left to the bulge of an outcrop of boulders where a crowd of cawing, mean-eyed crows strutted impatiently, waiting on their turn for the tasty leftover pickings. Must be the prospect of some meal, he pondered; maybe a stray steer come to grief, a lame horse put out of its misery, a mountain dog crawled away to die. Big meat for hungry beaks.

He grunted again and swallowed on the noisy rumble of his stomach. 'Food', he murmured, belching on the nip of hunger pains. Time to eat; time to go find himself something; anything, damn near anywhere would do. But, hell, he thought, out here in a nowhere land? Some chance, some hope! So maybe he should get back to the main trail, see what morsels he might hunt down far side of the rocky crags to the east. Get to being curious like the buzzards and trust he got as lucky.

'Hell!' he grunted, and had half-reined his mount to the trail when the crack of wings, the squabbling cawing of the crows halted him again, this time with a sudden trickle of cold sweat in the nape of his neck.

Last time he had heard birds scavenging like that had been out Scarcut Creek, day they had flushed out the last of the Billy Dance gang, moved in to pick off the remains of the murderous scum and bring Billy in

13

to stand to his trial at Forman. Only thing they had left to the birds that day had been bodies. . . .

Two minutes and a quick surge of his mount later, John Kavanagh had reached the boulders, scattered the birds and discovered the decomposing body of Joe Blossom.

Fellow had been dead some time, judging by the stench and state of him. Shot clean through, four bullets, close range, easy as hitting a barn door at six paces; no chance either, poor devil's hands had been tied, roped like a steer to a branding.

Kavanagh grunted, swallowed and moved slowly, carefully round the rotting mass. So just who, in God's name, he wondered, had come to sinking this low? More than one of the scumbags; ground hereabouts was scuffed real rough. Who, and why? This had been no straight stand-off, no gun to gun showdown, fairly drawn with the odds level placed till one proved faster than the other. No reckoning to the rules.

No, this had been an execution.

Kavanagh spat across the path of a strutting crow, glared at a perched buzzard and shuffled a pace closer to the body. One-time decent pants, he noted, soled and heeled boots – quality leather too – tailored shirt, fine cloth, and some belt there . . . good as new, carved buckle, made to order. Fellow had shown some taste.

Well, now, he pondered, squatting up wind of the stench, shame to leave a belt that good to the pickings of just any passing drifter. Belt hardly worn to the first crease of leather would fetch a good price – meal of fresh steak, apple pie to follow, and maybe more than once if he held to a tight deal. Steak, pie, beer. . . . Hell, this was no time to get fussy!

Kavanagh drew the belt gently on the tips of his fingers from the mass, grimacing at the slither of dead flesh, the crack of congealed body liquids and blood as they oozed to the movement.

'Nasty,' he grunted, gritting his teeth against the final tug that drew the belt clear to the dirt. Still, he reflected, comes the need, comes the deed . . . and, what the heck, fellow was hardly going to find use for a belt, be it Heaven or Hell he had headed!

Kavanagh came slowly to his full height, the belt hanging loose in his grip, took a long, last look at the body, turned and walked back to his horse.

Came to something, he reflected, mounting up, when a man got to lifting the pickings from a dead body for the price of his next meal. Came to something else when he did so without a qualm, or the ache of his conscience, and could ride on without a second thought for who the fellow might have been, how it was he had come to dying such a miserable death.

Did not stop him pondering, however, who had brought him to that end in the manner they had. Or why.

Kavanagh reined the mount round to face the body and the squawking strutting mass of gathering birds. Poor devil had been shot through as if to a countdown, a roar that might have sounded to be one gun. But there had been four shots, all separate, spread even from a line. Four shots, four guns . . . four men who had known precisely where they would do the killing and had chosen the dirt track off the main trail because they had known it was there, somewhere remote and lost where your everyday travelling man would rarely stray.

Maybe they had figured on it being weeks, maybe months, before the body was discovered, if ever. Maybe they had chosen the dirt track for that very reason. Four men who had known the place and how to reach it, precisely how long it would take to get here.

Local men.

Kavanagh drew the mount round again, urged it to the track, up the slope to the main trail, and halted, his gaze piercing the glare ahead. Trail ran straight for a half-mile, then swung away to the lift of a sprawling bluff; pine outcrop beyond it, backdrop of high and already snow-capped mountain peaks where the light lay clear and bright. Clear enough to see a finger twist of smoke no more than a couple of miles distant.

No saying as to the habitation, he thought, easing the mount on, but maybe it would be welcoming enough to trade a meal for a barely creased new belt.

Or say who it was had worn it.

Three

Lily Hassels swung her legs from the couch in Doc Brands' parlour, hitched her pants to her still trim waist, buttoned her shirt and thrust her hands to her hips.

'Well?' she asked, with a toss of her yellow hair to her long, smooth neck. 'What's the verdict? Still good for a month or so?'

'You'll do,' said Doc, drawing back the drapes on the fiercely bright afternoon beyond the window, 'but it's a deal more to luck than judgement, Lil, and that's the truth of it.' He turned from the glare with a resigned shrug of his rounded shoulders. 'Yuh want it straight? Yuh'll get it, anyhow! Another six months leadin' the sorta life yuh got back there at the Best Bet, and yuh won't be worth more than the price of planked pine. I'm tellin' yuh, woman your age—'

'I'm twenty-eight and not a day more!' protested Lily with a wry smile.

'Yeah, and fast pushin' forty state that body of yours is in!' Doc Brands sighed, raised an inquisitive eyebrow from its grey bushy mass and crossed to the cabinet at the far end of the room. 'Yuh want my advice – *again?*' he croaked rummaging among the bottles on the cluttered cabinet shelves.

'I heard it a dozen times already,' said Lily, reaching for her broad-brimmed hat. 'One more time ain't goin' to hurt none.'

'Time yuh pulled out, Lil. No messin', no half measures. And I mean *out*. Get clear of Tove, the company he keeps, that damned saloon, the town. . . . Just out, far as yuh can make it. Some place where yuh ain't addled through with booze and cigar fumes, where yuh can get to a decent square meal a day, where the air's clean, the livin' fresh, and there ain't a whole queue of two-bit drifters hoppin' in and out of yuh bed like jackrabbits at a prairie hoedown!'

'Tell me about it,' murmured Lily, turning the hat through her hands. 'But some chance, eh? Heck, Doc, you know the score for me well enough. I'm tied into Tove tighter than a tick to an armpit 'til I got that debt to him cleared in full. And yuh know what that means.'

'I know, I know,' grunted Doc, still rummaging. 'Tove's got yuh roped same as he has the rest of the girls back there, and I wouldn't set no store to yuh ever payin' up in full to the way of his thinkin'. Payin' back in hard cash is one thing: in kind, it don't never get cleared. Hell, who's measurin', anyhow?' He selected a bottle, studied the label and weighed it carefully in his hand. 'Only time Tove's goin' to release yuh is the day he sees yuh can't stand, and even then—'

18

'That for me?' asked Lily, nodding to the bottle. 'Magic potion to keep me awake, or somethin' to close my eyes permanent?'

'Ain't no cause for talk like that, not in my surgery there ain't.' Doc eyed the label again. 'I tried most things on yuh, and that's a fact. Clean out of options right now, but this,' – he held the bottle to the woman's view – 'this is somethin' from way back. Old Comanche medicine.'

'Indian medicine?' grimaced Lily. 'Gettin' desperate, aren't we?'

'Now don't you go underratin' this. Ain't a deal the Comanche don't know about stayin' right side of that big plain in the sky for as long as they can. I know, I seen it. Time I was out the high country back in forty-eight—'

'So what the hell is that stuff?' frowned Lily.

Doc fumbled deep in a pocket for his spectacles, flipped them one-handed to the bridge of his nose and peered closer at the scrawled writing on the label. 'Made this up a while back ... but that ain't to say it ain't still workin' ... some of these Comanche medicines stay potent for a whole year and more. Anyhow, like I say, made this up with yourself in mind, matter of fact. Figured there'd come a day when I'd need it.'

He grunted, peered closer and cleared his throat importantly. 'In ordinary folks' language, it's an elixir, somethin' to pep yuh up, give yuh a lift, at the same time, well, relax yuh. Should sleep a deal easier.'

'Doin' a helluva lot there, ain't it?' said Lily, moving to Doc's side to read the label. 'What yuh put in it exactly?'

'Oh, touch of this, spot of that. Nothin' to go frettin'

over. Just keep taking it, twice a day 'til it's through, then come and see me again.'

'Well,' murmured Lily, weighing the bottle in her hand, 'you're the doc. Guess yuh know best. Girl's gotta put her trust some place, 'specially in a town like this.' She sighed and smiled softly. 'Thanks, Doc, you're a friend. Wouldn't have gotten this far without yuh. Two bits to my best garter, I'd have been worm meat long back. Speaking of which—'

'I know what you're goin' to ask, and the answer's still the same: no, I ain't seen hide nor hair of Joe Blossom since the mornin' he rode out with Tove and his scum friends. So mebbe you're right – he's been worm meat ever since. Wouldn't take no bets against it.'

'But if that's the case, it'd be murder. Not one of them rats got good cause to go killin' Joe. What did he do, f'Cris'sake? Nothin' that anyone he was tied in with hadn't.'

Doc removed his spectacles, folded them carefully and slid them to his pocket. 'Mebbe it's what he *hadn't* done, or *wouldn't* do, that marked him out. Yuh get to nestin' with rats, yuh play rat. Ain't no room for conscience.'

'You mean him bein' tied in with the McLey killin'?' said Lily.

Doc shrugged. 'No denyin' it, is there? Happened by chance to be there the night Loafer pulled the trigger. But he went deeper, didn't he? Sided up along of Tove. Started runnin' with the same lousy pack.'

'But I don't figure it,' said Lily, crossing to the parlour room window. 'Joe might've gotten to havin' second thoughts, but, hell, so what? Ain't nobody in back of nowhere Wargrit goin' to bring him to book, is there? Ain't a soul in town unaware of Tove and his bunch standin' to the killin' of McLey. But who in hell's shoutin' about it? Who'd give a damn, anyhow? Who'd dare to give a damn?'

'So mebbe Tove's gettin' to some new plannin',' said Doc, fixing his hands tightly behind his back as he joined Lily and leaned forward to peer out of the window. 'Mebbe the rats have got to stirrin'. Yuh heard talk of anythin'?'

'Nothin',' murmured Lily in a near whisper.

Doc grunted and rocked rhythmically on his heels. 'When yuh seen as much of human nature as I have, yuh get to realizin' real fast that one bad turn soon leads to another. Tove ain't had much in the way of action of late, has he? Nothin' to scheme for, to plan on. So what's he plottin' now, and why ain't Joe Blossom a part of it?' His old boots creaked through a final rock to a standstill. 'What's so important to him it's worth killin' one of his own for?'

Doc Brands and Lily Hassels exchanged deep, questioning stares that might have lingered in the silence had it not been for the approach of tired hoofs through the dirt in the empty afternoon street, and the sight of the trail-scuffed, unshaven rider drifting into Wargrit like something from a long forgotten past.

It was a whole minute before Doc recognized the belt slung loose across the rider's saddle.

Four

Small town, neat enough and tidy; clean street, scrubbed boardwalks, no loose trash and nothing, at a first glance, out of place. Sort of town that settled an impression of being organized, thought Kavanagh, drifting slowly through the shadowed side of the street. Maybe too organized, he grunted to his watchful gaze. Awful quiet for the time of day; not a deal of coming and going; barely a handful of bodies to either come or go.

He nodded to the one-eyed glance of an old-timer seated in the cool veranda shade at the barbering shop, smiled softly at the woman hurrying from the well-stocked, newly painted mercantile, and winked at the open-mouthed youngster watching from behind the safety of a water butt. Folk were not much for greeting, he reflected. Or maybe just a mite suspicious of strangers. Could be there were not too many of them inclined to bother with a place as quiet as Wargrit.

So be it; that suited him just fine. A town where the folk stayed to themselves, would ask no questions and be content to let a dirt trail drifter do his drifting and pass on. But not before he had raised the price of a decent meal on the trade of the dead man's belt.

Saloon coming up on the right, he noted, narrowing his gaze on the lounging, heavily ironed fellow at the batwings. A cool beer would hit the back of his throat like an angel's breath, but the food would have to come first, so leave it, he resolved, move on to the eating-house, maybe a small hotel, assuming Wargrit got to boasting such a place.

Meantime, the lounging fellow at the batwings had been joined by a fancy-shirted, slick-fingered gambling type still shuffling a pack of cards. Sight of a new face in town sure aroused some interest.

Livery to the left, funeral parlour next to it – both deserted – smart, detached home in a fenced garden with a latch gate bearing the name plate *Doc. Brands, Physician* in clean-cut lettering – two faces watching from the window – the church spire lifting tall and white to the still bright blue sky, and then, tucked well back of a one-time gunsmith's and a dusty-windowed saddlery, the *Wargrit Eating-House: Rooms To Let.*

Do just fine, thought Kavanagh, reining the tired mount to the hitching rail fronting the clapboard bulk. Just fine.

'I ain't usually for no horse-tradin', mister, and that's straight up. T'ain't my way, never has been. Not that I'd see a fella go hungry, yuh understand. Nossir, wouldn't do that. All the same. . . .'

The nervous, twitchy-cheeked man brushed a shaking hand at the cow-lick of hair slipping over his eyes and drummed the fingers of his free hand over the desk counter in the shadowed reception of the rooming-house.

'So is that a "Yes" or a "No?" ' asked Kavanagh, shifting the belt an inch closer to the man's hand.

'Well,' began the man again, 't'ain't exactly a "No", but it ain't exactly an acceptance neither.' The drumming fingers fell silent. 'Where'd yuh get this?' he croaked drily, nodding at the belt.

'It matter any?' said Kavanagh. 'Here, there – don't change the value of the piece, does it? Custom-made belt of this quality's gotta be worth a meal. Wear it m'self if it weren't for the fact. . . . Well, that ain't of no concern. We for dealin' here, or ain't we?'

The half-open door to the room at the man's back eased a fraction wider as the lounging man at the saloon stepped from the darkness. 'Do the deal, Jake,' he murmured. 'Fella there looks in real need of a square meal.'

The man shivered, turned quickly and flicked at the cow-lick. 'Why, sure. . . . Sure, if yuh figure—'

'Just do it, Jake,' mouthed the man, a slow, wet grin breaking his lips, his gaze narrowing on Kavanagh. 'Yuh come far, fella?'

'Trailed out of San Apee day or so back,' said Kavanagh as he slid both hands to the counter.

'Main trail, or yuh take the long route?'

Kavanagh waited a moment, his stare tightening on

the lounger. 'Main trail,' he lied quietly. 'Didn't know no long route.'

'Oh, sure, there's a long route right enough,' blustered the shaking man with another flick at the cowlick. 'Trail's far side of Old Bluff. T'ain't no more than a dirt track, o'course. Sorta trail yuh'd expect a fella wantin' to stay outa sight to take. . . .' The man's voice slid to a hoarse, cracking whisper as a sudden sweat beaded across his brow.

'Yuh goin' to get to the cookin', Jake?' clipped the lounger through a fierce glance. 'Don't want to keep a hungry man waitin', do yuh?'

'No. . . . Sure thing. Get to it right away.'

'And, Jake, best throw in a room for the night for the man, I reckon. Belt of that quality is worth it.'

Jake fingered the cow-lick as he sweated through another shiver. 'Like yuh say, a room for the night. Number Four,' he stuttered, backing to the rear room.

'Obliged,' said Kavanagh, still watching the lounger.

'My pleasure, mister. Sometimes yuh just got to hurry this town along a mite. Gets to slowin' so much it ain't barely movin'!' The man's grin dampened to a gleam. 'Didn't catch yuh name.'

'Didn't mention it,' said Kavanagh, shifting his hands across the belt.

'I'll mebbe take that through to Jake, shall I?' grinned the lounger.

'No, do that m'self when I seen the meal – and the room,' smiled Kavanagh, lifting the belt from the counter.

25

'Suit y'self,' said the man, the grin fading.

'I usually do,' drawled Kavanagh, tossing the belt across his shoulder. 'Now, yuh hand me the key to my room back of yuh there?'

A wispy scattering of dust shimmered on the draught as the door thudded shut at Kavanagh's back. He blinked, seeking out the shadowed shapes of the room's furniture – sparse enough and broodingly indifferent to a presence – tightened his gaze on the single window where the drapes hung half-closed, then tossed the belt to the bed and stared at it as if seeing it for the first time again on the body of the dead man.

No question of it now, he pondered, whoever it was had taken the lead back there on the dirt trail had been local, a Wargrit man who had happened, by chance or choice, to be a sharp burr deep in somebody's boot – too sharp and too deep to be allowed to go on living. And two bits to a handful of beans, the lounging fellow had been one of the four whose guns had settled the issue.

Hell, he thought, leaning back on the door, his eyes closing on the shadows, hand-crafted belt of best leather with a carved buckle might fetch the price of a full square meal, but *not* with a room thrown in on the deal. Not unless whoever it was making the offer set a special value on the belt.

Kavanagh grunted and opened his eyes wide and gleaming. Only thing 'special' to the belt he had lifted from the dead man was the man himself and the grisly means by which he had died.

'Hell,' he mouthed aloud, pushing himself clear of the door and crossing to the window, last thing Wargrit had ever wanted to see again was that strip of leather. So just why was it worth so much in the hands of a stranger, and what was it hiding?

Somebody knew, somebody had spooked at the sight of it slung across a drifter's saddle, and somebody was sure enough going to one heap of trouble to make certain it stayed right here in town.

Somebody very like the lounging fellow there watching the window from the opposite side of the street, thought Kavanagh, twitching aside the gap in the drapes.

Well, now, he smiled, easing back to the shadows, maybe it was going to prove a whole lot interesting to see how big a meal it was he had traded.

Or how much of it he was expected to stomach.

Five

Cornelius Tove peered intently into the mirror as he fingered the delicate trim of his moustache, snapped loose a stray hair without so much as a wince and shifted his careful touch to the set and curl of his sideburns. Hint of grey there, he mused, half turning to catch the spread of pale lantern light in the private room of the Best Bet saloon; age creeping in, or was it the burden of his responsibilities?

His gaze slid to the reflection of the three men seated at the table behind him. Marcus Pitch, detached and nonchalant as ever, his only concern the run of the cards he dealt himself, his eyes steady and unblinking, unlit cheroot rolling easy in the corner of his mouth.

Jonas Bantry, sweating and twitchy, his gaze darting from face to face, to the tips of his fingers spread flat and fat on the green baize tabletop like caged birds looking for freedom, his gut bulging, timepiece chain stretched to the limit of its links.

And then Loafer, doing what he did best and was paid for: waiting on orders.

Barely a grey hair between the three of them, thought Tove, turning from the mirror, his hands smoothing the velvet-faced lapels of his tailored dress coat. 'So,' he announced bluntly, 'seems like we got a problem, don't it?'

'Yuh want my reckonin' on it—' began Bantry.

'Not yet, Jonas, not yet,' soothed Tove. 'Time ain't come for panickin'. We think this through. Put together a plan.' His hands slid away to his trouser pockets. 'How you seein' it, Marcus? Yuh givin' the matter some thought there?'

'Some,' murmured Pitch, his gaze still on the run of the cards.

'Well, if it ain't too much trouble and yuh can spare us the time—'

Pitch lifted his gaze sullenly and rolled the cheroot to a firmer grip. 'Simple enough to my thinkin'. Fella back there enjoyin' his meal took the dirt trail out of San Apee, stumbled across Joe Blossom and figured that belt of his worth the price of a meal. No harm to that, savin' he turned up here to trade it.'

'Precisely!' spluttered Bantry, his hands thudding the table. 'That's just it – he turned up here, and first person sees him with that belt will know exactly what happened to Joe and just who it was did for him. Don't take no figurin' from there for the whole darned town to get to thinkin' back to McLey, and once they start down that track—'

29

'Hold it, hold it,' clipped Tove, raising an arm. 'Yuh racin' on there some, Jonas. Too fast, too soon. You're panickin'. Only one who's dealt with the driftin' fella so far is Jake, and we all know Jake, don't we? Won't take no more than a little *persuadin'* from Loafer for him to keep his mouth shut. That so, Loafer?'

'Yuh got it, Mr Tove. Anytime,' grinned the man.

'That's all very well,' began Bantry again. 'But right now we're wastin' time. Ain't no sayin' who's got to talkin' to the fella. Could be somebody with him even as he's eatin'. Fella could be spillin' the whole story. And where in hell is that goin' to leave us?'

'In Hell, o'course,' drawled Pitch. 'Yuh just said as much.'

'Don't get smart—' snapped Bantry, his face shading to sweat-beaded crimson.

'All right!' croaked Tove, stepping closer to the table. 'That's enough, all of yuh. Now yuh listen up, hear what I'm sayin', get some sense into yuh heads before yuh've stirred up half the town with yuh rantin'.'

Marcus Pitch fanned the playing cards across the table.

Bantry ran a shaking hand over his face.

Loafer picked at a sliver of food lodged in his broken teeth.

Tove moved slowly round the table pausing at the back of each man, staring into the top of his head as if reading the thoughts in his mind. 'Fact,' he began, his hands tight clenched behind him, 'the fella's here, he's got the belt, but he ain't goin' nowhere. We took care of that, didn't we? Fact, so now that we got him penned at Jake's roomin'-house, what do we do with him?'

He paused, waited, listened to the slow tick of the clock from a dark corner, moved on and began again: 'I'll tell yuh exactly what we do – we kill him, no messin', no fuss. That way we get the belt and silence any chance of the fella tellin' how he came by it.' He paused again. 'Hell, who in this world is goin' to miss some dirt-bagged drifter who probably ain't had roots and nothin' of kin since he was knee-high to a steer? Driftin' types are ten to the dollar anytime, anywhere. Scrape 'em off yuh boots like yuh would the dirt. Ain't that so, Loafer? You seen the fella down there at Jake's; you talked to him. Ain't I right? You tell 'em.'

Loafer slapped his lips, licked the tooth-probing finger and leaned back in his chair. 'S'right, Mr Tove, I seen him. He ain't nothin' save bein' in need of a square meal.'

'Yuh could take him out? No trouble?' gulped Bantry.

'Not a spit,' grinned Loafer.

'There yuh are, then,' smiled Tove, releasing his hands to settle them on his lapels. 'Problem solved. Give the fella the satisfaction of his last supper, so to speak, then Loafer'll get down to Jake's soon as the poor devil's tucked between the sheets, do what's necessary, retrieve the belt and we can all get back to settlin' the final plannin' for the stage due here in a week. That suit yuh all? Yuh happy now, Jonas?'

'Well, I got to admit I'd sleep a whole lot easier if I

knew for certain that belt was burned or buried some place,' said Bantry, wiping the suddenly chilled sweat from his face. 'And like yuh say, if the fella ain't around to get to talkin', well, now—'

'I seen the fella,' said Pitch quietly, scooping the playing cards from the table. 'I saw him ride in.'

Three pairs of eyes flicked anxiously to the gambler's face, where the expression remained implacably frozen.

'So?' croaked Tove.

'So, like I say, I seen him.' Pitch shuffled the cards and began to deal face up to himself. 'Rides tall, easy in the saddle. Soft hands. Packin' a useful Colt.' He halted the deal at the ace of spades. 'Bet he knows how to use it too,' he grinned.

'That's fool talk, Marcus, and yuh know it,' dismissed Tove, tightening his grip on his jacket lapels. 'I ain't never seen no drifter yet could spread six shots to the same target.'

'Even so . . .' pondered, Bantry, blinking on a fresh surge of sweat.

'Just get to it, Loafer,' snapped Tove hurriedly. 'Let's get this business done before we start seein' ghosts or some such damn silly thing. Yuh get over to Jake's right now, yuh hear? Do it, get that belt and put the fear of death into anybody crosses yuh. Understood?'

'Got yuh, Mr Tove,' said Loafer, scraping back the chair as he came to his feet. 'All through in an hour,' he added, patting the bulk of his holstered Colt.

'Just watch for his eyes,' murmured Pitch, dealing another card.

Loafer had left the room, Tove turned again to the mirror, and Jonas Bantry buried his face in an already sodden bandanna, when Pitch dealt the joker. But the clock in the corner striking ten drowned his thoughtful grunt.

Doc Brands consulted his pocket timepiece, checked it against the clock on the front parlour wall, turned down the glow of the lantern light to a soft blur, and went quietly from his home to the shadow-filled street where only a lone dog scavenging for its supper gave him a second glance.

Ten-thirty, he pondered, stepping quickly through the barely moonlit night towards the dark mass of Jake's rooming-house. Could be he had left it a mite late; fellow could be sleeping; worse, he might have pulled out, left town on the back trail East. Unlikely, he mused, not unless he was in some big hurry, and that was not the impression he had given as he had drifted in. No, this fellow would be for making the most of Jake's generosity.

'Moonshine!' he muttered under his breath, as he paused a moment to peer at the seemingly lifeless house. Jake had acted on orders from Loafer to give the fellow a meal and hold him in town for the night on the luxury of a free bed and clean sheets.

'Jake wouldn't argue with his shadow, let alone Loafer!' Lily Hassels had reported back to Doc having established where the drifter was holed up. And the belt, Doc had asked, had it been recognized? 'Must have,' Lily had reckoned. 'Tove, Pitch, Bantry – any one of 'em could've spotted the fella ridin' in. Loafer's only their messenger, but he's spelled out Tove's orders clear enough. Jake ain't for arguin'. Fella's traded the belt for a square meal. Bed comes as a bonus. Might as well be the poor devil's coffin! They'll kill him t'night, yuh can bet on it.'

Not if I got a say in it, thought Doc, hurrying on to the house. Tove had got away with the shooting of Sheriff McLey on the threat of what would follow if so much as a finger was raised against him. Doubtless he had settled with Joe Blossom for some equally dark reason. But if he figured now on murdering an innocent man in his bed. . . . 'No chance!' he muttered again, slipping silently to the rear of the house where it was known across town that the door was never locked.

But on this night, in the creeping chill of an already settling frost, it was. Locked, with not a hint of light from the narrow gap at the foot of the door, and not a sound to be heard behind it.

Doc might have been tempted then to hurry on, try the front door, seek out a partially open window, do whatever he could to raise Jake from his slumbers, get to warning the drifter before it was too late.

But maybe it was, anyhow, he groaned, lifting his boot from the seep of sticky blood on the doorstep.

Six

Doc Brands had fallen back, his gaze still fixed on the thickening seep of blood, a cold sweat tingling in the nape of his neck, when a scuffle somewhere in the rooms above him narrowed his eyes to probe the dark sprawl of first-floor windows.

Somebody up there, sure enough, he thought, turning quickly to stumble to the side of the house and the front porch door. 'Jake!' he called on a croaked, cracking voice. 'Jake! Yuh in there?'

Silence. Nothing save the hiss of his breath, the beat of his heart.

He reached the porch, lunged his full weight at the door. Locked and bolted. 'Damn!' he cursed, falling back again, gaze spinning now over the faceless windows. 'Jake, f'Cris-sake! What the hell's goin' on in there?'

He had his answer in the ripping snarl and blaze of gunfire. Two fast shots from a Colt, a gurgled, strangled moan, something half-mouthed, and then the shattering splinter of glass showering across the night and the plunging mound of a body hitting the dirt with a sickening, crunching thud.

Doc had only to take a short step closer to be certain that Loafer had breathed his last before he hit the ground, shot through with carefully aimed, deliberate lead. The gunslinging sidekick had barely had the time for fingers to brush the butt of his Colt.

Doc was moving again, this time with his shoulder braced for an impact with the door that would force it open, when he stumbled, lost his balance and sprawled across the shards of broken glass at precisely the same moment as a hissing rush of flame licked across the windows of the first-floor rooms like the masks of leering fire dancers.

'Sonofabitch!' he was moaning, when somebody, in a suddenly growing mêlée of legs and boots and scurrying shapes behind a screeching babble of voices, grabbed his legs and dragged him clear, face-down through the dirt.

'Will somebody, any-goddamn-body, tell me just what in hell is goin' on here?' Tove strode up and down the line of townsfolk standing in awe of the still blazing rooming house, the sweat gleaming on his face, his arms waving, body tensed with nerves, eyes flashing hawk-like over the stares of the bemused men and women. 'Well, ain't nobody got a voice?' he yelled. 'You there—' He grabbed a dusty-faced, bent old-timer. 'What yuh see? What happened, f'Cris'sake?'

'I ain't a notion of how it got started, Mr Tove, and that's the truth of it,' croaked the old man, shrugging off Tove's grip. 'Time I got here along of the others place was goin' up fast as a prairie fire. All's I know is they found that fella Loafer there shot through and dragged what was still left of Jake from the back. Hell, yuh know what – somebody had cut his throat.'

'S'right, Mr Tove,' called a man. 'Seen it m'self.'

'Me too,' shouted another.

'Who the hell started the fire?' piped a youth from the back of the crowd.

'Yeah, who did that?' sneered a pot-bellied fellow rocking on his heels. 'That ain't none of Jake's doin'. That's your man, Mr Tove? He start it?'

' 'Course he didn't,' croaked Tove. 'What'd he want to do a thing like that for?'

'Weren't never any sayin' to what Loafer did, was there?' sneered Pot-belly again. 'I once seen him—'

'Watch yuh goddamn tongue there,' flared Tove, his stare deepening.

'The crowd eased back at the splintering collapse of timbers and surge of flame.

'Ain't nothin' to be saved there,' said the old-timer shielding his watery gaze.

'Burn itself out come first light,' grunted a man, wiping the sweat from his face.

'I wanna know—' began Tove again, but fell silent under the slap of Pitch's hand to his arm.

'Leave it, for God's sake,' urged the gambler. 'Don't get y'self in deeper.'

'He's right,' shivered a sweat-soaked Jonas Bantry at Pitch's side. 'We're in deep enough,' he hissed. 'Damnit, we all of us know what happened. It was that—'

'Shut yuh mouth!' growled Tove. 'First one who gets to—'

'I said leave it,' urged Pitch again, tightenting his grip on Tove's arm. 'If yuh want to know more, get over to Doc's place. I hear as how he was spotted headin' this way before the fire got started.'

Tove's stare hardened, his expression unflinching at the spit and crackle of more falling timbers.

'What I want to know is where's that damned drifter now?' gulped Bantry.

'I'll tell yuh where he ain't,' mouthed Pitch. 'He ain't in that inferno there.'

'So where is he?' shivered Bantry.

Pitch peered into the depths of the night beyond the curtain of flames. 'Anywhere,' he murmured. 'Anywhere that's close, that is.'

'And the belt?'

'Where do yuh think, Jonas? Figure it.'

'Did yuh see anythin'?' whispered Lily Hassels at Doc Brands' shoulder. 'All I heard was the shootin'. Next thing the whole place was goin' up in flames.' She shuddered and pulled the shawl nervously across the cleavage exposed by her skimpy dress. 'Hell!' she hissed, snuggling closer to Doc, her gaze wide and staring from the deep shadowed veranda fronting the physician's home.

'Yuh ain't dressed for the occasion,' murmured Doc, watching the lick and dance of flames at the far end of the street.

'Workin' girl, aren't I?' grinned Lily. 'Leastways I was, 'til this.' Her gaze followed the flying swirl and crackle of a shower of sparks. 'Well,' she whispered again, 'did yuh see anythin'?'

'Nothin',' said Doc quietly. 'Blood at the back door – must've been Jake's. Heard somebody in one of the upstairs rooms; then nothin' 'til the shots, Loafer hitting the dirt at my feet, and the flames. Wasn't reckonin' on much from there on 'til somebody was pullin' me clear.' He winced and cradled a throbbing elbow in his hand.

'That fella – the drifter – he do all that?' asked Lily, shuddering again.

'Weren't the fairies, was it?' said Doc. 'Know what I reckon? I reckon Loafer came down to the house with orders from Tove to take out Jake and the drifter and get the belt. He got to Jake all right, but he was a whole sight too slow for the drifter.'

'Yuh figure he's left town?' frowned Lily.

'No hint of his mount anywhere, so he must have.'

'And the belt with him?'

'I'd bet on that,' said Doc.

'So we've mebbe seen the last of him?'

'That ain't such an easy wager. Fella ain't that dumb not to realize there's a whole lot of somethin' special about that belt. Mebbe he's curious. Mebbe he'll want to know. Mebbe he's figurin' for what he took from Joe

Blossom's body bein' worth one helluva deal more than a square meal. And mebbe, just mebbe he's sufficiently down on his luck to want to know precisely what it'll buy – and, more to the point, who's payin'.'

Doc grunted and rubbed his chin thoughtfully. 'And so would I, Lily, so would I.' He turned quickly to face her. 'Yuh get back to the saloon, yuh hear'? And once you're there, yuh got a real job of work to do. Find out all yuh can, from wherever yuh can, about whatever it is Tove's plannin'. Use any means, but find out.'

'Any means?' grinned Lily.

'Best yuh got,' said Doc, fingering the shawl into her neck. 'Might be yuh last chance.' He smiled and patted her cheek. 'Get to it – and keep takin' the medicine!'

'Meantime,' whispered Lily, glancing over Doc's shoulder. 'yuh got company. Tove and Pitch headin' this way.'

'Right on time,' murmured Doc, without turning. 'Don't let 'em find you here. Now scoot!'

Lily Hassels had disappeared into the swirling shadows of the flame-dazzled night, and Doc Brands settled himself in the rocker on his porch, when Tove flung open the latch-gate and strode down the path to the veranda, snorting fire.

Seven

Three miles due north of the town of Wargrit, at the end of a rough country trail that peters out to thick pine forest on a sweep of foothills, lie the snowcapped peaks of the Crowfoot mountains.

Come late Fall, with the northerly winds biting deep and the creek streams shrinking in the grip of frost and ice, the first snows have already settled and a new silence hugged the land to sleep. Few men risk these parts at this time. Who would take the choice of cold, lean cover and scant resources save those in need of some place to hide and stay hidden?

John Kavanagh had, and reached the first straggle of a pine outcrop at sun-up following the night of the fire at the Wargrit rooming-house.

His plan, as he reined his mount into shelter against the whip of the thin morning wind, was simple enough. No frills, nothing fancy, he would make the most of what he had and continue north, high into the Crowfoots and hopefully beyond them to the lusher plains before winter took its final hold.

Wargrit could stay right where it was – behind him!

That, at least, had been the plan, and still was even as he checked out his few belongings and figured how best to use them in the month's trek to come through the mountain trails and passes.

Who needed Wargrit, anyhow, he mused, fingering the patched and darned leanness of his bedroll? The town had provided a sound, square meal, his best in a long time. Sure it had, but at a price: a price as high as it ever came.

Two men dead: the twitchy, nerve-racked rooming-house proprietor, his throat slashed in a cold-blooded murder by the lounging man with the bad teeth; and the lounger himself a corpse not a half-hour later.

Kavanagh had grunted loudly to himself at the rec-ollection. Hell, had there been a choice back there in the musty, shadow-filled room? Kill or be killed, no side measures, no quarter. The lounging man had been too slow, too sure that his target would be sleeping.

And all for the need to bury the secrets of a dead man's belt.

What was it with that belt, the dead man on the dirt trail, the whole damned town, that so worried some-body deep enough to kill for? Time had been when John Kavanagh would have shifted Heaven and Hell for the answers. But all that had been years ago. Shame about the fire, though, he had sighed, but necessary for the town to stay occupied while he had made good his escape.

Only decent thing to come out of Wargrit had been the last of it.

And with that the episode might have ended in the cold, snow-drifted foothills of the Crowfoots and John Kavanagh taken to the trail to the high peaks, had it not been, once again, for Joe Blossom's belt.

Kavanagh's resolve had been for throwing it away right there and then. It had served its purpose. On the other hand, he had pondered, it might do so again when he finally cleared the mountains. If it had been good for a meal in Wargrit, it would fetch its price in the first plains' town he hit. Always assuming he was permitted to get that far.

He had taken the belt from his saddle-bag, turned it thoughtfully through his fingers, traced the fine design work, weighed the buckle in the palm of his hand. A sick-scared rooming-house owner had bled to his death for it, a two-bit gunslinger stood to his inflated ego for it, a roped, unarmed man been dragged to a dirt trail corner and shot for it; somebody back there in Wargrit had not given a damn for the life of John Kavanagh in his desperate need for it.

And there was no good reason to suppose he had given up. . . .

There were no fresh tracks through the snow to the high peaks of the Crowfoots on that morning.

'We need men, horses. Guns. And we need 'em fast. Now!' Jonas Bantry rolled like a greasy ball round the table in the back room of the Best Bet saloon, one finger digging deep into the tightness of his collar, another scything the air to emphasize his words, his voice cracked, eyes bulging. 'Yuh got it all organized?' he snapped, his wet gaze flat on Cornelius Tove. 'We ain't got too much time.'

Tove examined his trimmed, manicured fingernails uninterestedly and silently, his only gesture to the storekeeper being a quick glance beyond him to where Marcus Pitch broke the seal on a new pack of cards and began to shuffle them.

'That sonofa-driftin'-bitch ain't got more than a few hours start on us,' continued Bantry, rolling on to the softly shadowed end of the room where he paused to flatten a hand on his gleaming bald pate. 'We put some men together now and they could be into the mountains come noon. Hell, fella ain't goin' to make any fast ridin' this time of year, is he? First snow's fallen, ice is packin' in . . . he won't make Pine Pass 'til sundown. We get to him there, finish the job, retrieve that damned belt, and . . . well, town ain't goin' to fret that long over Jake and his place burnin' down, are they? Few drinks on the house here, give it a coupla days and they'll forget. Damnit, might even get to handin' out free candy at my store.'

'Generous,' murmured Pitch, his concentration on the cards.

'Most,' added Tove, spreading his fingers for inspection.

Bantry wiped a sweaty hand across the seat of his trousers, sighed and rolled his eyes to the ceiling. 'Beats me how it ever came to this,' he moaned as if address-ing the sudden appearance of a higher power. 'A down-and-out gets lucky, stumbles across Joe, takes his belt, rides into town . . . and, presto, the world goes mad! Loafer fouls up a straight killin', Jake's dead, spend half the night fightin' a fire, and that damned drifter still rides outa here quiet as a Sabbath. Beats me!'

The storekeeper lowered his gaze and stared vacantly round the room where the frail morning light lay like old breath. 'Should never have sold Joe that belt, o'course. See that now. Point is,' he shuddered as if coming awake, 'we got to make sure that drifter don't go no further with it. He gets to handin' that belt to some law-puncher and tellin' the tale of how he came by it, and that'll be it – the whole damned thing'll spill in our laps and there won't be no plan for the stage. Chances are we'll all hang for McLey.'

Bantry looked up fiercely. 'So what yuh doin' about it? Yuh got the men, the horses, the guns?'

'Yuh all through there?' said Tove, thrusting his hands into his trouser pockets.

'I surely hope so,' muttered Pitch.

'All I want to know—' spluttered Bantry.

'I sent for Prince,' said Tove flatly. 'Had one of the boys ride for San Apee at first light. Prince'll be here t'morrow sundown. That suit yuh?'

'But that'll be too late,' groaned Bantry. 'We need to move now, today.'

'Don't never see further than yuh poky nose, do yuh, Jonas?' sneered Tove. 'If that drifter makes it into the

Crowfoots it'll be weeks before he hits a town and we'll be long through here. If he's fool enough to show his face hereabouts again, Prince'll take care of him. He don't come cheap, but he's worth five of Loafer.'

'And he watches a fella's eyes,' quipped Pitch.

'But supposin—' began Bantry again.

'Do yuh supposin' some place else, Jonas,' said Tove, crossing to lay an arm across Bantry's shoulders. 'Yuh just leave this to Pitch and me, will yuh? We got the whole thing in hand. Now, yuh take my advice, yuh'll go and avail y'self of the pleasures of Lily out there. On the house, eh? Tell her I sent yuh.'

'Well,' sweated Bantry, 'I ain't so sure. . . .'

But by then Jonas had been ushered from the room and Tove closed the door on him and settled his hands flat on the table at Pitch's side. 'Goin' to have to watch him real close,' he said quietly.

'Same as we are that Doc,' clipped Pitch.

'Hmmm,' murmured Tove. 'I fancy Mr Prince is goin' to earn his money.'

Lily Hassels twisted a finger through the fall of a curl, stood back from the mirror and swirled the folds of her long skirt. Not bad for an early morning start after a hellish night, she thought, pausing to stare at herself. She had looked worse, even on a good day.

She adjusted the set of the dress across her shoulders and crossed the room to the window overlooking the street. Town looked as exhausted as she felt. Still a drift of smoke there from the burned-out rooming-house, and the smell of it. . . . She sniffed; charred timbers, scorched belongings, the stench of death. She shivered. Place was locked into silence as if at a funeral that no one knew how to end.

She looked carefully along the shadowed, empty street to where it drifted away to the trail to the mountain range. Was that the track the stranger had taken in his getaway, she wondered; torched the house and then made a dash for it while the town spun into panic? Was he there now, making his slow way into the ice and snow-gripped Crowfoots, glad to have put Wargrit behind him, but still pondering how it was it had all begun with a dead man's belt?

Safest and wisest thing the fellow could do now was keep right on going, deep as he could bury himself in the bleak sprawl of creeks and passes. And the belt would go with him. He would never know the story of the man who had worn it, or why Cornelius Tove had passed a death sentence on Joe Blossom.

But maybe she would. . . .

'You bet,' she murmured, moving back to the mirror. She gave the curl another twist, swirled the skirt, patted her hips and turned to the door. Time for some action, she thought, stiffening her shoulders. Time to go see if the old magic would work on Jonas Bantry even at this unearthly hour.

What was it they said about the early bird?

Eight

Lily Hassels had reached the deserted bar of the Best Bet saloon from her upstairs room at almost precisely the moment Jonas Bantry had left Tove's private quarters. She had spoken quietly to him for a half-minute before taking his arm and crossing the street with him to his still locked and shuttered store. The 'Closed' notice had stayed where it hung behind the dusty glass.

Marcus Pitch had chanced his luck on a game of Patience without bothering to give Cornelius Tove, preening himself at the mirror, a second glance. The game would be over and another started long before Tove was all through counting grey hairs.

Doc Brands had shaved and washed as best he could against the aches and bruises in his tired limbs and limits of his concentration. He had a head full of questions and precious few answers.

Where was the drifter now? Had he headed deep into the mountains; would he keep going? Tove had lost Loafer – at no great cost by his standards – but would he replace him? Would it be necessary for whatever he was planning back there at the Best Bet with Pitch and Bantry? Would Lily get close enough, and be persuasive enough, to discover the plan, if in fact there was one?

Tove's mood the night of the fire had been part confusion, part anger, two steps short of shooting up the town, save for the restraining hand of Pitch and Doc's calm refusal to say anything, or be riled. Tove could rant all he wanted, Doc had decided, but not on his front porch.

'Suggest yuh move on, Mr Tove, go settle yourself with a drink or somethin' before I get to bringin' a charge of trespass!' he had warned from the depths of his veranda rocker.

Tove had left, and Doc waited till he was out of sight before mopping the sweat from his brow.

No saying what a man like Tove might come to, though, in his frame of mind and with a town already spooked through to jump to his every snap.

Not that everybody was for jumping, thought Doc, slipping achingly into his jacket as he crossed to the window of his front parlour. Frank Packet, Jake's brother, for one.

Frank was in a mood apart on this morning as he rummaged like a man in a trance through the charred, smoking remains of the rooming-house. No bets on what was going through his mind, mused Doc, as he watched the man turn over the few identifiable scraps of flotsam from his brother's life. Jake might not have been much of a fellow to stand up to the likes of Loafer and Tove, but, damn it, he had been blood kin, born right along of Frank there at the old Packet homestead a mile out of town.

No man worth a spit settled easy for his brother dying to the flash of a knife at his throat in the hand of a two-bit gunslinger with bad teeth. And certainly not Frank Packet.

Somebody should go comfort him, leastways listen to him, before his thinking festered to a prospect of real trouble.

But Doc was a few steps too slow, a minute too late as he opened the door to his porch to halt Frank Packet in his quietly determined stride down the street, through the early morning reach of shadows and the lifting glare of the blood-red sun, towards the Best Bet saloon.

And Doc's half-mouthed call to him died on a croak.

'Tove, yuh in there? Yuh going to step out, give me the time of day? Frank Packet here. Yuh know me well enough. I want words with yuh, and I want 'em now. Yuh hearin' me?'

The man swayed and rocked on his heels in his straddled stance in the deserted, silent street, his voice cracking and wheezing like the boughs of an old tree bending to a wind, his stare fixed, steady and wide on the bat wings to the saloon bar.

'I ain't armed. Ain't carryin' no piece. I ain't lookin' for no trouble with yuh, just want some answers. Wanna talk this through, man to man, so's we got it straight. Yuh hear?'

Doc Brands had crossed the street from his porch to the shadowed boardwalk opposite and sidled softly towards Bantry's store facing the saloon, his gaze tight on Frank's every move and gesture. Fellow was lathering himself up some, he thought, understandably so in his natural grief. But if he figured for one moment that Tove was going to step through those batwings in full view of the whole town for some cosy, consoling chat, he had best figure again, and fast.

'I'm waitin',' shouted Frank, stumbling a step to his left in his uncertain balance. 'I ain't got all day. Things to do . . . a whole heap of 'em, not least the fixin' of a funeral for what I got left of Jake back there.'

Frank swayed again, stumbled, righted himself to as near upright as he was ever going to get. He was sweating now, noted Doc.

'Yuh goin' to pay for Jake's pine box, Mr Tove? I reckon yuh should. Figure for that fire bein' your fault, sure I do, but weren't the fire that did for my brother, was it? Nossir, it was not.' Frank wiped the sweat from his face. 'Who was it slit my brother's throat? Who was it? Answer me that. And don't say yuh can't. Your man was there, weren't he? That no-good scumbag, Loafer. He slit Jake's throat, or are yuh sayin' it was that two-bit drifter holed-up there? Which one of 'em, Mr Tove? I'd sure as hell like to know!'

Hold on there, Frank, thought Doc, narrowing his gaze on the batwings. You get to pushing this too far

51

and somebody will have the job of burying you alongside your brother. He swallowed. No movement in the
bar that he could see; nothing at any of the windows.
Place was as silent, as brooding as Boot Hill on a wet
day.

Frank staggered a few shuffling steps closer to the
saloon's shadowed veranda. 'Hey, yuh listenin' in
there?' he croaked. 'Anybody hearin' me? I got a right
to be heard. You bet I have. Ain't nobody goin' to shut
Frank Packet's mouth 'til I got some answers.' Another
stagger, another sway; a blinking of wide, red-rimmed
eyes, as bloodshot as the fierce morning sun.

First hint of movement, noted Doc, far end of the
street; group of fellows, four or five, watching, waiting,
listening. Young boy there scurrying to the safety
behind a pile of wooden crates side of the store; woman
hesitating, shopping basket clutched close, too scared
to come on, too curious to turn back.

'Tove,' yelled Frank, 'I'm waitin'.'

And he is going to let you do just that, thought Doc,
gulping as his gaze narrowed to a squint on the merest
shift of a shadow beyond the batwings. One of the pot
men, one of Tove's sidekicks, a bar girl? Too early for
the drinkers, even whispering Pete, the town drunk.
Had Tove moved, or was he. . . . Hold it, the shape in
the shadow was closing on the 'wings.

Unless he was much mistaken, that was Marcus Pitch.

It was, trim and tailored as ever in his crisp laun-
dered shirt, pressed pants, fitted jacket, polished boots,
the inevitable deck of cards dancing in his long fingers,

his gaze sharp as a blade beneath the broad-brimmed hat, a soft, condescending grin at his lips.

And a Colt strapped tight to his side.

'Ain't for discussin' this with you, Pitch,' sneered Frank, thrusting back his shoulders. 'Not unless yuh tied into it.'

The playing cards flicked through Pitch's fingers. 'Why don't yuh just leave this, Frank?' he said, his stare shifting quickly to Packet's face. 'Mr Tove'll see yuh right. Yuh ain't no cause to get frettin'.'

'No cause?' flared Frank. 'No damn cause? I'll say I got cause, all the cause a fellow needs! That's my brother lyin' blood-soaked back of the undertaker's. Ain't he cause enough?' Frank swayed through a stumbling step. 'You just stand aside there and let me get to Tove. I ain't settlin' for nobody else.'

'I think not,' murmured Pitch, the cards gathered tight in his left hand. 'This ain't the time, and this ain't the place. Call it a day, shall we?'

'Over my dead body!' groaned Frank.

'Precisely,' grinned the gambling man.

The two shots from Pitch's gun split the morning silence as if ripping parched canvas into halves, spinning the defenceless Frank Packet like a top across the street to finally sprawl face-down and lifeless in the sun-glazed dirt.

Pitch had holstered the Colt again and tossed the deck of cards to the ground before the batwings creaked and Tove stepped to the boardwalk, his face expressionless, stare fixed on the dead body, the fingers of one hand working absent-mindedly at the curl of hairs in his sideburns.

And nobody in that street or at a window overlooking it who had witnessed the murder of Frank Packet dared to so much as catch their breath.

Nine

'How far did yuh get before that sonofabitch shot Frank?' Doc Brands laid a warm, gentle hand on Lily Hassels' arm and stared intently into her eyes.

'Far enough,' said Lily, easing back in her chair at the table in Doc's parlour as her eyes closed tiredly.

'Hell, I know this ain't easy, Lil,' soothed Doc, 'and I'm the last to be askin' it of yuh, but yuh can see the way things are goin'. If we don't—'

'Tove's sent for Prince,' clipped the woman, her eyes opening wide and bright. 'And yuh know what that means, don't yuh?'

'Boden Prince,' groaned Doc. His hand slid away from Lily's arm. 'Hired gun. Works out of San Apee. They don't come any worse in a count of gunslingin' scum. But, hell, he don't come cheap neither. If Tove's spendin' that sorta money, he must be plannin' on somethin' big.' The hand reached for Lily's arm again. 'Bantry get to tellin' yuh?'

'Would've got the whole thing if Frank hadn't lost his

head like he did. As it is. . . . Seems like there's a stage due here next week.'

'A stage?' frowned Doc. 'We ain't had a stage through Wargrit in three years, not since they opened the trail South of Pine Pass.'

'Yeah, well, that's just it. Trail outa the pass flooded two months back, and it ain't fit to be worked these comin' winter months, so the line's re-routin' 'til next spring. Stage'll leave the Crowfoots on the eastern trail and head for San Apee through Wargrit. First one'll be here three days from now.'

'But what's so damned special about a stage?' frowned Doc again. 'Special enough to kill Joe Blossom for, murder Frank Packet, send for Boden Prince to gunsling for yuh? Some stage, eh?'

'That much I didn't learn,' sighed Lily. 'But like yuh say, some stage – or a very special somebody ridin' it.'

Doc was silent for a moment as he came to his feet and crossed the room to the framed map of the territory on the wall at Lily's back. 'Stage out of Springfield,' he began, a finger tracing the spidery trail route, 'headin' south. First stop the swing station at Baker's Rock, then on to Feather Creek; out of the Creek, and then – ah, yes – turn east for Mission Forks and you'd be makin' Cookstown in, say, two days. Another day and, yep, I got it right here, Lil, pick up the old track through the Doon Drift and it's a straight run clear through to Wargrit. Whole trip done and dusted, Springfield to San Apee, in five days at most.'

Doc turned from the map. 'Know what I figure? I

reckon for that stage hittin' Wargrit about noon one day next week, mebbe Tuesday.' He tapped a finger on his chin. 'Nothin' to that. T'ain't exactly a world event, is it? So could be yuh right, Lil. Could well be that Tove's interest in the stage's arrival concerns who's goin' to step down from it in the hour it'll take to rest and water up.' He paused, blinking. 'Ain't no way of knowin', is there? Not unless—'

'Not unless I can wheedle it out of Bantry,' said Lily, coming to her feet wearily.

'Reckon yuh can?' asked Doc.

'Do my best, if yuh think it'll help.' Lily stretched, yawned and patted the falls of her hair. 'Back to work!' she smiled. 'But even if I do get Bantry to tell all, how's it goin' to help? Ain't goin' to be a deal we can do about it, is there, not with Prince rulin' the roost as he will be by then? T'ain't information we need so much as a fast gun. That's about the size of it, Doc.'

Doc sighed as he turned back to the framed map. 'That is exactly the size of it,' he murmured in a cracked, hoarse whisper. 'I just wonder where that driftin' fella is right now. . . .'

It was in the early evening of that same day that a handful of men, for the most part silent, darkly mournful of the moment, but quietly resolved and determined, gathered in the dusty, deserted, one-time saddlery in the shadow of Jake Packet's burned-out rooming-house.

If they had a common cause in the secrecy of their meeting, the hushed, quiet talk among themselves, the tendency to hug the shadows beyond the pale glow of the light from a single lantern, it was not apparent. They might have been ordinary town men meeting on an ordinary night to chew over no more than ordinary, everyday matters.

Not so, as would have been seen the minute Elias Macks stepped to the centre of the pool of light and called respectfully for the men's attention.

'Ain't no point in talkin' too deep into this,' he began, his eyes clear and bright in their steady gaze. 'We all know why we're here. We all seen enough: Jake's place there, his body like it was; the shootin' of Frank, an unarmed man gunned down in cold blood, and we all know them at the root of it – same scum who like as not have killed Joe Blossom and probably did for Sheriff McLey.'

There was a murmur of agreement among the watchful gathering.

'I ain't for mincin' my words when I say we been livin' along of this without a murmur among us. Just taken it, turned a blind eye, said nothin', done nothin'. And that don't stand none to our credit, not mine, not yours, and not one mite to the womenfolk and young 'uns we got to our charge. Say it any-which-way yuh like, we stand in the shadow of our shame.'

'Harsh talkin' there, Elias,' grunted a man.

'Mebbe,' said Macks stiffening. 'Truth has a habit of fallin' that way. Still, that's as was. Time's come to right a few wrongs here.'

'Say that again,' murmured a man in the corner.

'It'll be the doin' of it that counts,' added another to the nodding of heads.

'Like yuh say,' grunted Macks. 'Well, I been givin' some thought to that. Seems to me this whole thing's come to a head with the ridin' into town of that stranger, whoever he was. Talk has it he was carryin' Joe Blossom's belt. Mebbe he was, but t'ain't relevant now, is it, not with him long since disappeared into the Crowfoots like as not? And I ain't for bankin' on seein' him again.'

'Not if he's got any sense, we won't!' chipped a man with his back to the door.

'So,' continued Macks, 'we go this alone, no messin', no dancin' to the principles of it, no moralizin', no second chances. We clear this town of Tove, Pitch and Bantry, and we get to it sun-up. Agreed?'

'All the way!' said a tall man, moving closer to the pool of light. 'And I personally ain't for keepin' it tidy neither!'

The men nodded, murmured, patted the fellow's back.

'Hang 'em, if that's what it takes,' growled the man in the corner.

'All right, all right,' gestured Macks, 'we're all of a mind, no doubtin' to that. Now comin' to the detail—'

'Mebbe somebody should talk to Doc,' said an oldster, examining the bowl of his pipe. 'Can't see as how we can leave him outa this. And what about Lily? She ain't done nobody no harm. Her and them girls got a livin' hell back there at the Best Bet.'

'See yuh point there, Adam,' said Macks, 'and I'll look to it soon as we're through here. Now, to them details. I figure it like this. . . .'

Long before the lantern in the one-time Wargrit saddlery had been doused and the gathering of men dispersed silently to their homes through the chill Fall night, a lone rider, clearing the last of the long miles from San Apee, had come within view of the moonlit outskirts of the town.

Boden Prince had settled his immediate business hurriedly on receipt of the message from Tove. The money on offer for a job Prince reckoned he could handle with 'one arm tied behind his back' was too good to miss. Watching over the pale-faced, skulking residents of a town – most of them too gun spooked to breathe, let alone get to taking any action – while Tove and his sidekicks got to whatever it was they were about, would be as easy as feeding beech nuts to hogs.

No problem, but maybe with just enough 'amusement' on the side to keep him happy and his gun hand loose while he waited to collect Tove's handsome payout.

And so it was that Boden Prince had ridden promptly and well ahead of schedule for his appointment with the generous benefactors of Wargrit.

Thirty miles distant, directly to the north of the San Apee trail where winter was already stalking cat-like through the foothills of the Crowfoot mountain range, a second lone rider was also making his way towards

Wargrit through that same chill night.

Unlike Boden Prince, John Kavanagh was in no great hurry to reach the town, save for the prospect of a warm fire, and he harboured no particular incentive to hurry him along. Sun-up, noon, late afternoon, the town would still be there and he would still be the drifter with the dead man's belt. And somebody, no doubt, would still be waiting to take it from him.

Time, he had always reckoned, was of little note when the counting of it came to spanning no further than the next day.

Two riders closing on Wargrit, one from the south, one from the north, with nothing in common between them on that night save the town itself.

But that, come a few short hours, was going to prove more than enough.

Ten

It was somewhere into the dark iciness of the early hours when Lily Hassels dared to stir herself from the snoring bulk of Jonas Bantry.

She was a full five minutes easing from the bed in the still smoky room above the store, putting her bare feet to the boards and slowly, delicately, like a bewildered moth feeling for the light, finally coming upright and crossing to where her clothes lay in a crumpled heap on a chair.

She dressed quickly, stifling her shivers against the cold, one eye on the sleeping mound, conscious of its every twitch. Two more minutes, she thought, struggling with the buttons of her dress, that was all she needed; two minutes to be fully dressed, out of the room and fumbling her way down the stairs to the back door. Another five, once clear of the store, and she would be waking Doc Brands with the bad news.

She fixed the last button, smoothed the long skirt, patted her hair to position and crept on tiptoe to the door.

Bantry snorted, rolled, twitched his nose and resumed the steady snoring.

Lily's hand fell to the doorknob, gripped it, turned it through its annoying click and held her breath as the door creaked open.

Two steps, a moment's pause as she closed the door softly behind her, and she was moving easily down the corridor to the stairhead to the back door. She winced at the groan of a warped stair, steadied herself and moved carefully on.

Almost there. Bantry was still snoring. The night hung like a curtain. Somewhere a clock chimed the half-hour. She stifled a gasp at the sudden dart of a mouse. Probably a darned sight more scared than she was, she grinned, concentrating her gaze on the back door.

It opened to the softest squeak of tired hinges, the draught of cold air through the gap sending a shudder through Lily's tensed body. She waited, swallowed, narrowed her eyes on the freezing darkness, then inched her way carefully onto the cluttered porch piled high with crates, barrels, filled and half-filled sacks, the flotsam of a working store.

All quiet. Nothing moving.

She slid between two crates, paused again, listened – and shivered, gulped, watched the swirl of her breath hang like a cloud for what seemed forever as the soft swish of hoofs, jangle of easy tack broke the silence like the steps of ghosts.

Lily had slunk to the deepest cover of two stacked

crates and crouched almost to her knees by the time the black shapes of horse and rider passed in startling silhouette through the shimmer of moonlight at the far end of the street.

'Boden Prince,' she hissed. She knew the set of those shoulders, the pinched profile beneath the broad-brimmed hat, easy hands to slack reins, well enough. No need for a second glance as the rider passed heading for the Best Bet saloon.

He was early, she thought, watching him drift to the shadows – a whole sight too damned early. Hell, if she had reckoned on the pillow-talk news she had extracted from Bantry being bad, Prince's arrival had turned it to a mire.

The night was silent and empty again when Lily slid from the cover and headed for the clapboard bulk of Doc Brands' home.

She was shivering to her bones when he opened the back door to her nervous tapping.

'Of all the sons-of-goddamn-stupid-bitches, they gotta be it!' croaked Doc, hustling Lily into the clinging comfort of a blanket. 'I ain't never heard of anythin' so fool-headed. Yuh sure, absolutely certain?'

Lily nodded through a twitching shiver.

'Elias Macks leadin' the townsmen against Tove and Pitch?'

Lily nodded again and huddled deeper into the blanket.

'Here, get to the stove, my girl,' urged Doc, leading

her from the kitchen door to the range. He seated her in a chair, sighed and worked his fingers through a slow massage of her shoulders. 'And Tove knows about it. But how? Don't tell me, I can guess. Some rattler with a twisted mind figurin' for gettin' into Tove's favours. Misguided fool. . . . Still, that ain't the issue.' His fingers came to rest. 'With Prince in town this early, it'll be a bloodbath. He'll gun 'em soon as spit in their eyes, every last one. And Tove won't lift a finger to stop it.'

'We should try to stop 'em,' shivered Lily.

'Snowball's chance in hell,' groaned Doc. 'Yuh get men wound up for a killin' and they ain't never satisfied 'til they're through with it. Macks won't be listenin' to nobody, and when he does it'll be too damned late.'

'Even so—'

'Even so, I'll try – for what good it will do.' Doc's hands rested on Lily's shoulders as he moved round to face her. 'Much as I'd like to take care of yuh here, Lil, yuh goin' to have to get back to Bantry before there's a wink of light. Ain't a deal more yuh can do save stay close and keep yuh ears and eyes open – and yuh head down when it comes to the shootin'. Don't go riskin' nothin', yuh hear? Ain't nobody goin' to thank yuh for that. Town's set its trail and it'll hold to it now come hell or high water.'

Lily came unsteadily to her feet. 'When I first heard the scuff of them hoofs out there, I thought for a moment it might be. . . .' She shivered again. 'No such luck, eh? He's gone. The drifter's pulled out.'

'Well, mebbe he has at that,' said Doc, rubbing the

back of his neck. 'Though sometimes I ain't so sure, 'specially when I get to itchin' like I do.'

'Suggest yuh don't get to scratchin' too hard!' smiled Lily.

Cornelius Tove eyed the gunslinger carefully through a drifting haze of cigar smoke and wondered how it was he had the impression the fellow's stare was on him even when it seemed settled some place else. Maybe it was a trick that marked the man out. Maybe that was why you were never sure just who was watching who.

'Good to see yuh again, Boden,' he grinned. 'Been a long time. Amarillo, wasn't it? Had ourselves a time there, eh?'

'Pickstown,' drawled Prince, his gaze lurking somewhere beyond Tove's shoulder. 'It was Pickstown we had a time. Yuh were drunk last I saw of yuh in Amarillo.'

'Pickstown – 'course it was. Anyhow, still good to see yuh. And right on time, as ever. That's what I like about you, Boden, yuh got a knack of turnin' up at just the right time.' Tove turned to Pitch seated at the baize covered table in the bar's private room, a deck of cards flicking through his fingers. 'Ain't that so, Marcus?'

'Always,' murmured Pitch, without disturbing his concentration.

'And we got some trouble comin' right up. First light, I figure.' Tove dusted the lapels of his jacket. 'Nothin' yuh can't handle, Boden. Handful of town men gettin' a touch above themselves. Reckonin' on disturbin' my place here. But you ain't goin' to let that happen, are yuh? I want them hotheads taught a lesson, harsh as yuh like, just so's they don't get to figurin' on a repeat performance. Sort of thing you do best, eh?'

Only one eye seemed to shift in Prince's steady gaze.

'We also got a driftin' man,' said Pitch, watching the play of the cards as he dealt them.

Prince's gaze shifted the merest fraction.

Tove gave the lapels a final dust and gripped them tightly. 'That ain't of note,' he snapped irritably. 'Some dirt-trail scumbag drifted in here to cause a spot of bother, but he's gone, ridden out. Somewhere deep in the Crowfoots by now. Just a two-bit drifter. Nobody to set any store by.'

'Savin' that he took out Loafer, torched the roomin'-house and spooked half the town,' clipped Pitch, still dealing from the cards in his hand.

'Yuh get a name?' asked Prince, the gaze moving slowly to Pitch.

'No name,' said the gambler. 'Never said one and didn't stay long enough to be asked twice. Trailed out of San Apee, hit town, and left leavin' a long shadow.'

'Well, now, that ain't strictly true, is it?' protested Tove. 'I mean, put like that anybody'd get to thinkin' the fella was some sorta threat or somethin'. Hell, like I say, he was a two-bit drifter. Seen their kind a hundred times. Here t'day, gone to the dirt tomorrow. You've seen 'em, Boden, sure yuh have. Probably gunned more than you've stepped over, eh?'

'Tall, straight-backed, sat his mount easy,' murmured Pitch. 'A real good-lookin' Colt strapped to him.'

'Sure, and yuh get them types too,' huffed Tove. 'Probably lifted the gun from some corpse, same as he did that belt.'

'Corpse?' frowned Prince. 'What corpse? What belt?'

'Best get to tellin' the man, hadn't yuh?' said Pitch, flicking his gaze to Tove. 'Don't want Boden here walkin' into trouble, do we?'

Tove fumed quietly.

Prince's stare settled everywhere.

Eleven

There was the faintest smudge of first light to the east of Wargrit when Doc Brands struggled wearily into his jacket, set his hat tight on his head and left his clapboard home with the neat latch gate and made for the darkest shadow to hand.

Too early yet for men to lather themselves to a killing, he decided, making his way quickly through the frosty morning air to the tumbledown homes at the back of the one-time saddlery. Be a whole hour before Elias Macks rallied his party for the showdown with Tove. They would wait for the late Fall sun to glare low in the empty skies and the first wisps of smoke from newly riddled and stirred stoves to lift like fingers before they gathered, took their orders, and then moved slowly, silently to the Best Bet saloon.

Plan would be to lure Tove to the boardwalk fronting the bar before he was fully awake. They would figure for Pitch, and maybe Bantry, standing to him, but three against a majority of the town's able-bodied would be no match.

They might hope for Tove backing down – he was always quick to reckon the odds – and agreeing to leave town. Pitch would not be for gambling on a stacked deck. Bantry would bluster, switching sides and loyalty with only the preservation of his own greasy skin as the first consideration.

What Macks and his men would not have reckoned for was Boden Prince. They would neither be ready nor in any state to react instinctively to a gun that would blaze first and leave the questions for later.

Doc hurried on, passing the saddlery and the charred remains of the gutted rooming-house with no more than a cursory glance and a shake of his head. He was facing Elias Macks' single-storey home when he paused, caught his breath against the thin chill, and turned his gaze to the distant bulk of Bantry's store, wondering if Lily had made it safely back to the room where Jonas heaved and snored in contented sleep.

Or had he stirred and ordered Lily back to his bed? She would maybe figure it safer all round to keep him there.

Doc reached Macks' front door, tapped lightly and waited.

A slow tread, a pause, click of a gun hammer and then the door was open and Doc was being ushered quickly into the low-lit, smoky room.

'What the hell yuh doin' about at this hour, Doc?' snapped Macks, holstering the Colt.

'What do yuh think?' blinked Doc against the half light. 'I heard what yuh plannin', and I'm tellin' yuh now—'

'Too late for a lecture, Doc. Town men are of a mind to settle whatever it is we got plaguin' us. Ain't no goin' back.'

'Well, yuh might just get to revisin' that somewhat when yuh hear what I got to tell yuh. That gunslingin' sonofabitch out of San Apee, Boden Prince no less, is in town. Right now. And I don't have to tell yuh whose company he's keepin', do I?'

Macks stared, grunted, licked his lips. 'Boden Prince, eh?' he murmured. 'Gettin' serious, ain't it? Must be somethin' real big brewin' for Tove to go to that sorta expense.'

'You said it,' croaked Doc. 'But Tove ain't the issue here; it's Prince yuh gotta worry about. Ain't a man among yuh, not one in the whole town, could hold his own to the scum, let alone take him out. And he'll be waitin' on yuh, sure enough. He *knows* you're comin'. Yuh got a loose tongue among yuh. So if yuh want my advice—'

'Ain't seekin' it, Doc,' said Macks, putting his back to the door. 'Grateful for what yuh told me, o'course, and know yuh mean well, but if we back off now there ain't never goin' to come another time. What's gotta be done is goin' to be done. Wouldn't be a man for turnin' from it.'

'And how many will die for it?' asked Doc, a beading of sweat glistening in his frown. 'Yuh bothered to ask the

71

women who's for losin' her man; the young 'uns who'll
give up a pa? Yuh put that to the town? No, yuh ain't.
Well, don't yuh think yuh should? I sure as hell do!'

Macks bit his lower lip and stiffened. 'It's survival
we're talkin' here, Doc. Town's gone rotten, and yuh
know it, same as I do. Same as we all do, damn it. Ain't
a man restin' easy in his bed for the fear of Tove and his
company. No sayin' to where they're leadin' us, but we
had a fair sample of it so far, ain't we? Sheriff McLey, Joe
Blossom, now Jake and his brother, Frank. Who's next?
Where's it all headin'?'

He spat into the palm of his hand and wiped it clean
on the seat of his pants. 'It's time for a reckonin'. Only
decent thing to stand to us so far is that drifter takin'
out Loafer. Wish we had the fella here right now, whoever he is. Still. . . . We'll manage. And we ain't for
turnin' back on the threat of Boden Prince. Mark that!
Not that there's cause for you to be involved, Doc. You
get back to doin' what yuh do best. We're mebbe goin'
to need yuh.'

'Yuh can bet on that!' grunted Doc. 'Sure yuh can –
I'll be there to pronounce on the dead, mop up what's
left of the wounded, tend the widows, comfort the
young 'uns. . . . Oh, sure. Good old Doc Brands!' he
scoffed and pulled at the brim of his hat. 'You're a fool,
Elias Macks, and there ain't for sayin' other. But, same
as all fools, yuh'll go on addin' to it, and there won't be
no stoppin' yuh. Now, if yuh'll stand aside there I'll bid
yuh good mornin'. I got a bag to pack – tight as I can
fill it with potions and bandages!'

There was still an hour to full light breaking when Doc stomped back to his clapboard home, banging the latch gate shut behind him.

The pants were too small and too tight and the gut a whole heap too prodigious to squeeze into them. In fact, when you came to seeing it this close, from this angle, mused Lily, stretching her legs the full length of the bed as she propped herself on one elbow, the sight of Jonas Bantry getting into his clothes was almost as ludicrous as watching him struggle out of them.

'Time I lost a few pounds here,' wheezed the store-keeper, closing the pants with a grunt.

'Never,' smiled Lily, stifling the onset of a giggle. 'Fine figure of a man, Mr Bantry. And I should know. Why, I seen fellas half your age wouldn't come within a spit of yuh.'

'Nice of yuh to say so, Lily,' grunted Bantry again, reaching for his fancy waistcoat, 'but I see what I see and I ain't for foolin' none.' He crossed carefully to the window, tweaked the drapes a fraction, and scanned the empty street below. 'What yuh see is mostly what yuh get in this life,' he murmured, squinting closer. 'Pays yuh to keep a sharp watch.'

'Yuh doin' plenty of that,' said Lily to the man's bent back. Yuh expectin' company; at this hour? T'ain't full light yet.'

'Them fool townsfolk,' croaked Bantry, still squinting. 'Time somebody taught 'em a lesson or two.'

Lily squirmed and clenched a fist. 'But, surely, it

73

don't call for you to get involved, Mr Bantry, does it?' she puffed. 'Not now, when we hardly got started.'

'Don't tempt me, gal. I might just weaken!' He let the drapes fall back, smiled and winked and shrugged himself into his jacket. 'But don't you move, yuh hear? Yuh stay right where you are, and soon as this business is done, I'll be back. Within the hour.'

'Well,' pouted Lily, slipping from between the sheets and crossing the room to the table, 'if yuh must, I suppose yuh must. Meantime, I'll just help m'self to a little drink here.'

She emptied the dregs of a whiskey bottle to a glass and put it gently to her lips, her gaze narrowing on the storekeeper as he turned to the window again and shifted the drapes for a view.

'Come on, come on,' he muttered, scanning the street from left to right. 'We ain't got all day to wait on this. Anybody'd think—'

Jonas Bantry would have heard nothing of the slow, measured step at his back, seen nothing of Lily's raised arm, the whiskey bottle clenched tight in her grip, and probably sensed nothing untoward or in any way different in the gently lifting light of day he had not seen in the hundreds before it. Not until it exploded and the morning was suddenly blindingly white and then hopelessly black might it have occurred to him that he had seen the last of it for the time being.

But by then, it was too late and he was already slipping to the floor at Lily's feet, the blood from the gash in the back of his head staining the threadbare carpet.

'You're wrong, Mr Bantry,' smiled Lily to herself. 'Sometimes what yuh see ain't what yuh get!'

Three minutes later she was dressed and rummaging through the storekeeper's wardrobe for the loaded Winchester she knew he kept hidden in its clutter.

The full light was breaking sharp and clear, shafting the shadows of the main street to stark black sentinels, when Elias Macks led the town men of Wargrit from the one-time saddlery through the crisp morning air towards the Best Bet saloon.

The group, a dozen or so strong, moved purposefully but steadily and silently, Colts holstered, rifles easy in firm grips, Macks at their head, his gaze fixed, expression taut.

Doc Brands, bag in hand, followed at a discreet distance, pausing only to urge curious onlookers to stand back, get into cover and 'Stay down, f'Cris'sake!' His more explicit curses he kept to himself.

The batwings at the Best Bet stayed as they always were at this time of day: flat, unmoving and lifeless.

Miras Carter, town undertaker, had dressed hurriedly into his sombre best and checked carefully over his stock of pine planking stacked in the lean-to at the rear of the parlour. Could get to being a busy day, he reckoned.

It had taken Lily Hassels only minutes to lock the door to Jonas Bantry's bedroom, pause for a moment at the head of the stairs to the deserted store, catch her breath, fix a loose strand of hair and slip quietly into the shadows behind the mercantile's bowed windows.

She had a clear view from here to the saloon opposite. If Boden Prince laid so much as a finger on the batwings. . . . She was getting ahead of herself, she winced, hooking the Winchester to a two-handed grip.

The shadows were still deep and heavy, the light beginning to glare in the strengthening sun as the town men reached the saloon, turned to face it and waited for Macks to be their spokesman.

His voice, when he found it, was cracked and hoarse, shards of glass under the heel of a boot, and broke that still morning's silence like the snap of a sudden wind.

'Don't need me to tell yuh why we're here, Tove,' he called to the empty boardwalk and the dark bulk of the building behind it. 'I'm speakin' for the town here. Every last man of it. Lookin' to hear some answers, same as Frank Packet was, and him without so much as a blade about him. Well, like yuh see, we ain't fool enough to stand unarmed – not that we're for firin' a single shot, not if this can be settled amicable. All yuh gotta do is step through them 'wings there. . . .

It was as the 'wings creaked apart and the tall, leather-booted shape of Boden Prince filled the space, Colts levelled and steady in both hands, that Elias Macks' voice drifted away and his mouth stayed open.

It was still open when the twin Colts blazed and the first man hit the dirt like a dropped stone.

Twelve

Nobody witnessing the blaze of Boden Prince's Colts on that morning, in the main street of Wargrit, had any clear recollection of just how many shots were fired. Some reckoned he emptied both chambers, some that it took only ten, in a rapid hail of spitting lead, for the blood to run as if the sun itself had bled.

But there was not a soul in any doubt of the body count and the damage inflicted when he was through and the silence descended like a shroud.

Four men flanking Elias Macks were dead before they had blinked; a fifth, dropping his rifle and turning to run, had been shot in the back. Macks was sent sprawling, one hand crimson with the spread of blood at his shoulder. A gangly limbed man screamed his agony as he gripped his thigh; another had his weapon spun from his hold and could only stare in stunned disbelief at his shattered hand.

Of the town deputation Macks had led from the saddlery minutes before, not one returned fire, or barely moved, until Prince strode to the boardwalk steps, the

Colts smoking but still levelled in his grip, and glared over the faces watching him like a hawk selecting its next easy prey.

'Are yuh for any more?' he drawled, his eyes seeming to be focused on a distant space. 'Or shall I make it a clean sweep?'

Those with their weapons still frozen between numbed fingers let them fall to the ground. A weedy, thin-faced fellow, all floppy hat, baggy shirt and patched pants, choked on a surge of vomit, spat violently and fell to his knees. An old-timer growled and threw his pipe to the dirt in disgust.

Somewhere out of the sight of Prince, a woman sobbed uncontrollably. A door banged. A sash window thudded shut. A horse snorted. A lone dog howled.

Prince's gaze flicked like a light to where Doc Brands waited in the shadows on the opposite side of the street.

'You the sawbones hereabouts?' he called, gesturing a Colt. 'Then yuh'd best get busy. The place is a mess!'

It was not until Doc had reached the first of those still breathing, that the batwings creaked open again and Cornelius Tove, Marcus Pitch at his side, stepped to the boardwalk and gazed over the carnage, his quick swallow lost in the ruffles of the cravat at his neck.

'All through, Mr Tove,' grinned Prince, holstering one of the Colts. 'Yuh'll have no more trouble.'

Pitch flicked a loose card through his fingers. Tove swallowed again and stepped to the edge of the board-walk.

'Didn't plan for it to be like this,' he began, addressing the remnants of Macks' deputation, Doc Brands, the suddenly hovering undertaker and the scattering of those brave enough to venture nervously into the street. 'Didn't have to be. But, there, yuh get to meddlin' and the price comes high. So yuh all just clear this street, eh? Get yourselves out of it. And let this be a warnin', yuh hear? Mr Prince ain't no soft belly. One word from me or Pitch here. . . . Well, yuh all seen the outcome.'

It was at that moment, as Tove, Boden Prince and Marcus Pitch glowered over the drained, pale faces and the morning light began to spread in the slow climb of the sun, that Lily Hassels flung open the door of Jonas Bantry's store, stepped through it and, with her face screwed tight against the kick and roar of the Winchester in her grip, released a volley of high, wild shots in what she prayed was the general direction of the Best Bet saloon.

Prince fell back instantly, pushing Marcus Pitch unceremoniously through the batwings as if clearing the boardwalk of a pestering hound. Cornelius Tove, too shocked and surprised to move at the sight of Lily advancing on him, the weapon still blazing, was just seconds too late in making his dive for cover.

A loose shot, the last that Lily had the strength to hold to anything like straight in her quivering aim, caught Tove in the upper arm, spinning him round and back, directly into the path of Boden Prince gathering himself for a shot at the staggering woman.

Prince pushed Tove aside, sprang from the boardwalk to the street and was closing, Colt levelled, like a mantling hawk on Lily when the Winchester finally fell from her hands and she collapsed in a heap of dusty, creased dress and bedraggled hair to the dirt.

Prince dragged her to her feet, thrust his greasy, stubbled face to within a breath of hers, and grinned. 'Now if this don't make my day!' he hissed.

The late Fall sun had reached its zenith, burned off the frost, warmed the day through and settled into its slow slide behind the high peaks to the west by the time Wargrit got to standing back and catching its breath.

The street had been cleaned up to the best anyone knew how or had the stomach for.

Town undertaker, Miras Carter, had taken the dead to the parlour, his major concern being the immediate depletion of his stocks of pine measured along of the prospect – too damned real, as he saw it – of more bodies to come.

Doc Brands, after tending to the needs of the direst wounded where they lay, had spent the rest of the day cleaning up, patching up, binding, bandaging and comforting until his eyes were sore, his fingers aching and his body so weary he might have slept wherever he happened to be standing.

And lurking constantly at the back of his mind whenever he turned to the next bloody mess, were his fears for Lily.

Nothing had been seen of her, Prince, Tove or Pitch since the gunslinger had dragged her back to the boardwalk fronting the saloon, pushed her through the batwings and disappeared after her.

'Don't take too much figurin', though, does it?' the old-timer had growled. 'Shan't see nothin' of any of the scum 'til they're good and ready.'

Somebody said as how he had heard and then seen Jonas Bantry ranting his way out of his store – 'and nursin' one helluva sore head!' – before descending on the Best Bet mouthing curses faster than he could swallow.

Finally, in the late afternoon with the spread of dusk already burying the shadows, Wargrit lay back exhausted, drifting into a silence so fragile, so uncertain, it would have broken at the scratch of a mouse.

Nobody truly slept, save to doze through snatched, fitful moments of nightmare, but nobody was tempted to move either, so that long before the coming of night the town had slipped readily enough into mourning.

Doc Brands stirred from whatever had passed for sleep with the moonlight full in his face.

He came quickly to his feet from the chair in his front parlour, squinted at the wall clock beyond the pale glow of lantern light, and was reaching instinctively for his jacket with one hand, his bag with the other, when the noise somewhere in the back room spurred him to shift even faster.

'I'm comin', I'm comin',' he croaked, struggling into his jacket. 'Just give a fella time here, will yuh? Goddamnit, I been at it since sun-up. And that ain't your fault, I know, but right now I got more folk bleedin' and moanin' than one pair of hands can handle, 'specially when I get to reckonin' just how many years they been at it!' The jacket settled, collar twisted, across his stooped shoulders. 'Tell yuh somethin' else. . . .'

Doc hesitated, his gaze suddenly tight on the door to the back. 'You still out there, whoever yuh are? Don't fret none if it's payin' that's botherin' yuh. Day like we've had in Wargrit and I ain't for handin' out bills in a hurry. Pay when yuh can. We'll get to it. Whole heap of other things round here to get to first. Yuh still there?'

Doc had his bag in his hand, his hat set firmly on his head, and was crossing to the door to the rear when it opened slowly, creakily, swinging full and wide on its weary hinges to the dark space beyond.

Except that the space was filled. 'Well, I'll be damned,' murmured Doc, easing his bag to the floor. 'I hadn't figured. . . . None of us had. . . .'

The dirt-trail drifter stepped into the room and closed the door softly behind him.

Thirteen

'I got it all mapped out for you, Lily Hassels,' croaked Tove, wincing as he adjusted the padding of bandage at his shoulder, his glare tight on the woman seated in a corner of the private back room at the Best Bet saloon. 'Know what?' he winced again as Jonas Bantry helped him into his tailored frock coat, 'I'm goin' to hand yuh over to Mr Prince out there for his pleasure for the duration of his stay. That's what I'm goin' to do, beginnin' this very night. And if I hear so much as a whimper out of yuh, I swear to God I'll. . . .' He groaned as the frock coat settled to his shape. 'All right, Jonas, all right. No need for yuh to make a meal of it.'

'Yuh got lucky there,' said Bantry, standing back. 'Another spit to the right and she'd have plugged yuh straight through. Bitch!'

'Yeah, well, if you'd been payin' a sight more attention to the day comin' up 'stead of gettin' to friskin' again, it might never have happened.'

'She caught me unawares, f'Cris'sake.'

'With yuh pants down!'

'Nothin' like. In fact—'

Pitch slammed his deck of cards to the baize-topped table. 'Will yuh shut it, pair of yuh?' he snapped. 'Who did what, when, where, how, ain't of no account to nobody, least of all me. I'm a deal more interested in where we go from here.'

'Simple,' said Tove, turning to examine and preen himself in the mirror, 'we sit tight. Town's quiet, and it'll stay that way, thanks to Mr Prince. I don't expect a peep outa nobody 'til we're through with our business and we're ready to leave.'

'Hope you're right,' drawled Pitch, fingering the cards again.

' 'Course I'm right. Yuh were there, yuh seen what Prince did. Hell, there ain't a man in town who'd dare to raise an eyebrow to him, let alone a finger.'

'Loungin' about in the bar out there like he owns the place,' said Bantry. 'I don't want for him gettin' two sizes bigger than his boots. Fella of that nature needs to be watched.'

'Yuh got the job, Jonas,' grinned Tove. 'You watch Mr Prince all yuh want. Only next time we need a little gun power hereabouts, don't let him see yuh gettin' picky. Right? Mr Prince is his own man.' He glanced at Lily. 'As the lady here is about to find out.'

Lily fidgeted, ran her hands down the folds of her skirts and avoided Tove's glance.

'Yeah, and that's another thing,' began Bantry. 'I ain't

so sure about lettin' Prince have all his own way—'

'We ain't seen nothin' of that driftin' fella,' murmured Pitch from the table.

'Ain't likely to, are we?' sneered Tove. 'He's long gone. If he weren't already deep into the Crowfoots, sound of Prince's guns would soon have put him there. No, we've long said goodbye to him.'

'Mebbe,' said Pitch.

'Wouldn't worry me none, even if he did show,' expanded Bantry, slipping his thumbs to the belt beneath his gut roll. 'Be just another body to Prince's account, wouldn't he? One word from us and – zing-zap – he's gone. That's what we pay for, ain't it? Good money for a fast gun.' He sighed and belched. 'And in our line of business of late, we need it.'

Pitch dealt the cards and did not lift his gaze from the table until the door to the bar opened and Prince stepped into the room. 'Yuh got a visitor,' he announced.

'Oh?' frowned Tove.

'The doc. Says he wants a word with yuh.'

'Show him in, Mr Prince. Show him in,' beamed Tove. 'He can take a look at this shoulder of mine while he's here.'

Bantry cleared the sweat from his face.

Lily shifted expectantly in the chair in the shadowed corner.

Marcus Pitch dealt himself a useless hand and was tempted to cheat from the bottom of the deck.

He did, and sat back satisfied.

Doc Brands' tired eyes, the droop of his shoulders, tight set of his lips in an expression of suppressed fury, said all that anybody needed to know of his mood as he moved ahead of Prince into the back room and heard the door click shut behind him.

He glanced quickly at Lily and nodded, then turned the full blaze of his stare on Tove. 'Yuh seen what yuh done to this town today?' he croaked, his eyes narrowing slowly. 'Yuh got any idea? Well, I guess not, eh? And even if yuh did, what's it matter? T'ain't you and yuh scum friends here doin' the shootin', is it? Nossir. Ain't goin' to mess like that. No blood on your hands – savin' McLey and Joe Blossom, Jake and his brother – leave the rest to Prince, can't yuh? He'll take out as many as yuh want. Anytime.'

Tove stiffened. Doc was conscious of Prince's breath, hot and damp, on his neck.

'Steady as yuh go there, Doc,' hissed Tove, sliding his hands to the lapels of his coat. 'Yuh might rate of some standin' hereabouts, but yuh ain't above bein' shown yuh place if it comes to it.'

'Want for me to finish it now, Mr Tove?' croaked Prince over Doc's shoulder.

'No, not yet, Mr Prince. Doc here's got a job to do. Best let him do it, I reckon.' Tove smiled gently. 'Yuh come here just to blow off, Doc, or did you have somethin' specific in mind?'

'Specific,' snapped Doc. ' 'Bout as specific as it gets.

We'll be buryin' the dead come mornin'. Whole town, or them's that left and got the guts for it, will be turnin' out to Boot Hill. Procession'll pass right by your place. Yuh might wish to pay yuh respects – but I wouldn't get too close if I were you. No tellin' the state of some folks' minds when they get to smellin' vermin.'

'Yuh made yuh point, Doc,' blustered Bantry. 'Yuh'd best leave now before somebody's temper gets to snappin'.'

'Do just that, Doc,' growled Tove. 'And right now.'

Doc grunted and turned his attention to the woman. 'Yuh all right, Lil?' he enquired. 'Don't let them abuse yuh none, yuh hear?'

'She's fine,' said Tove brusquely. 'Just go, will yuh?'

'Want me to look to yuh shoulder?' grinned Doc. 'Took a close thing there, didn't yuh? Could have been nasty.'

Tove stiffened again. 'Shoulder's fine. Flesh wound. Nothin' more.'

Doc shrugged and turned to face Prince at the door. 'Stand aside, mister. Some of us have real work to do.'

'Yuh see anythin' of that drifter?' piped Pitch from the green baize table.

Doc paused, his eyes narrowed, expression seemingly blank to his suddenly crowding thoughts. He swung round to Pitch. 'Only folk I seen this day have either been dead, dyin', or bleedin'. I don't recall no drifter bein' among 'em.'

'Just askin',' smiled Pitch, scooping up the playing cards.

Doc stared a moment, then grunted and turned back to the door.

'Goodnight, Doc,' began Tove airily. 'I'll mebbe see yuh at the wake, eh? See if I can spare the time.'

Doc was a full step short of the door when the sound of something hitting the floor in the deserted bar behind it silenced the room, save for the ticking of the clock and Boden Prince's slow, careful shuffle in his reach for the knob.

He opened the door just wide enough for a view of the bar, waited, listened, one hand slipping to his holster to draw a gleaming, long-barrelled Colt.

'Yuh see anythin'?' whispered Bantry, the sweat beading on his brow.

'Quiet!' snapped Tove.

Prince opened the door wide and slid into the bar, Doc Brands following in his steps. The room, only half-lit from a single, flickering lantern, had gathered the night to it in long, heavy shadows, deeper in the corners, stiff across the wall, lifeless where they sprawled from the bar to empty chairs and tables.

The boardwalk beyond the batwings was just as silent and deserted. Or was now, thought Doc, conscious of the others moving silently from the back room. Somebody had been out there in the street. Somebody who had crossed purposefully to the 'wings and waited just long enough to make the delivery that lay curled like a basking snake across the floorboards.

Joe Blossom's belt.

Marcus Pitch was the first to speak.

'Drifter didn't get far, did he? Must've taken a fancy to the place.'

Bantry sweated while Tove twitched and stared. Lily simply swallowed.

And Doc managed somehow to stifle his slow smile.

Fourteen

The frost that had settled in the still, icy air of the night took a while to thaw through the early hours of the following morning. It lay white and crisp and tight long after the sun had climbed above the high peak mountains and Wargrit had shivered and sniffled itself into life. Few were for stirring too soon. Some not at all given the option or a sound enough excuse.

Cornelius Tove, on the other hand, had not slept a wink. He had found himself a troubled, restless man, prone to pacing, preening, pausing to think, to ponder and to wonder at the root of it all, why the drifter had returned to Wargrit.

'Don't make no sense, does it?' he had argued to the watchful stares of Bantry, Pitch and Prince in the shadowy light of the back room. 'He'd gotten clear, hadn't he? Filled his belly, got the better of Loafer and ridden out. *And* he still had that damned belt. So what did he want to come back for, f'Cris'sake? And what's the point of doin' what he did? Why'd he toss the belt into the bar? Where is he now?'

'Waitin', I'd reckon,' said Pitch, stretching his arms behind his head and yawning.

'Just that,' nodded Bantry. 'He's waitin' somewhere out there, right here in town. You can bet on it. Hell, we don't know nothin' about him, do we? No name, no knowin' where he hails from, where he's plannin' to go. He could be anybody. Just anybody.'

'That still don't explain—' began Tove.

'He figures for havin' an edge, don't he?' said Pitch leaning forward to rest his arms on the green baize table. 'He knows there's a price on the belt – we made that plain enough – so he's curious, wonderin' how high it might go. He's a drifter, got no place special to be, so why not come back to Wargrit, try fixin' the precise value of the belt? What's he got to lose?'

'His life,' leered Tove, licking his lips, his glance straying to Boden Prince.

'We should've done it sooner,' said Bantry, beginning to sweat.

'Yeah, well yuh can blame Loafer for that.' Tove turned to the mirror. 'Point is, the fool-head ain't kept goin' has he? He's back, givin' us another chance.' He turned to Prince. 'Yuh'll handle that, my friend. No problem, eh?'

'No problem,' grunted Prince.

'Assuming yuh can find him,' croaked Bantry.

'He's hereabouts,' murmured Tove. 'I can feel it.'

Pitch reached for a pack of cards. 'I'd watch yuh back, Mr Prince,' he grinned, beginning to shuffle. 'Fella's packin' a tidy Colt. Driftin' types don't carry that sort of gun just for the look of it.'

Prince grunted, adjusted his hat, the set of his gun-belt and went from the room without another word.

'Now there, gentlemen, goes a professional. My kind of man,' smiled Tove.

Bantry sighed and closed his eyes.

Pitch played cards.

Lily Hassels pulled the blanket across her shoulders and moved carefully round the room to stand shivering at the side of the window overlooking the main street.

Quiet enough at this hour, she thought, watching the curls of smoke from the early fires. Nobody much for putting in an appearance, especially not this day, funeral day. Be a while yet before Miras Carter and his helpers loaded the coffins aboard the wagons for the short journey to Boot Hill. Doc would assemble the fol-lowers – those with the stomach and courage for it – and lead them silently, defiantly down the street, pass-ing the Best Bet saloon, and on to the bleak openness of Boot Hill, there to say a few words, a short reading, perhaps a hymn if there were any with a voice, before the slow walk back to town through the flat midday sun-light to the shadows of private grief.

She shivered, clung to the blanket and cursed qui-etly.

Damn Cornelius Tove – Bantry, Pitch and Prince right along of him! Damn Wargrit! Damn the whole godforsaken territory come to that! She brushed at a hot tear. Anything else worth damning while she was at it, she wondered? Sure, a long list of them, all the way from Wichita to Wargrit and back again!

She sniffed loudly, brushed at another tear and blinked. Then stepped back, stiffening.

Prince on the move. More of a prowl. Well, no second guessing what he was about.

The sight of Joe Blossom's belt tossed to the floor of the Best Bet's saloon bar had shaken them all, herself included, and it had been a whole three minutes before Prince had finally stopped circling it like some suspicious mountain lion and stooped to pick it up, hold it in his fingers to the shadowy half light and, along with the other unblinking eyes, simply stare at it.

Lily sniffed again and smiled softly to herself as she watched Prince sidle from the boardwalk shadows, cross the street and wait, pensive and watchful, at the side of Bantry's mercantile.

The sight of Joe's belt, and the means by which it had been delivered back to Wargrit, had frozen the blood in the veins faster than a dousing from an ice-packed creek stream.

Only Doc, it had seemed to Lily, had remained unmoved, as if expecting something just like this to happen, and right on time too. But only she, the Good Lord willing, had noticed his stifled smile.

So could it be, she had pondered, when Prince had finally come to lock her in her own bedroom, that Doc and the drifting man had somehow got together? She had dismissed the thoughts. She was getting a sight too close to clutching at straws.

Hold it, Prince was on the move again.

Lily pressed herself tight to the wall at the side of the window as she watched the gunslinger slip away to the next sprawl of shadow.

Tove and his cronies were taking the return of the drifter seriously. They wanted him gone, dead, and the sooner the better. Wargrit had to be theirs, severely under the thumb, every last living soul, by the time the stage out of Springfield made its unscheduled stop in just. . . . Lily frowned. How long? Another day, two? She had lost track of time.

Prince was still moving, making his way towards the spread of ramshackle barns, huts and long abandoned woodsheds at the back of the livery. He was figuring for the drifter being holed up at the trash end of town where nobody had cause to venture.

Maybe he was right. Fellow could hide in the shadows of ruins and the neglected for as long as it suited. She leaned forward for a wider view. Town was still quiet, waking slow and stiff to its day of mourning. Be a while yet before Miras Carter drew up the funeral wagons.

Prince had the town to himself. Almost. He could, of course, be sharing it with the drifter.

Prince had reached the first of the rundown shacks, paused, drawn a Colt, listened, watched, and moved on to the next ruin. Take him better part of a whole morning doing it this way, thought Lily, shifting again for a clearer view.

He had stepped momentarily out of her line of vision

when she caught the sudden glint from the shadows away to her right. She blinked. Trick of the light, or was there somebody there? Somebody who had just drawn his own Colt?

She felt the breath tight in her chest, a beading of sweat on her brow. Prince was in vision again and moving on. Nothing from the shadows to the right. Maybe she had been mistaken. Perhaps it had, after all, been a trick of the light.

No trick of the light. . . . Nossir, nothing like! There it was again, same place, same sudden gleam, and then gone. She would wager her last dollar there was somebody there, waiting, who had probably had Prince in his sights since the minute he had stepped from the boardwalk.

Too late now, Boden Prince, she grinned, as she watched him move stealthily, steadily on towards the shadows. Only a matter of time.

Or it would have been had something, perhaps the sudden scurry of a rat, not spooked the horses stabled in the livery.

The snorting, stamping of hoofs, whinnying as the fit of nerves spread among the mounts, the curling drifts of hot breath and steam from spooked, twitchy bodies, froze Prince where he stood with his boots no more than two steps from turning into a direct line to the shadows.

'Hell!' cursed Lily, pulling angrily at the blanket. Her gaze narrowed. Prince had not moved. The shadows, it seemed, had emptied.

It was a long three minutes before the stabled horses began to settle again. But how much of their commotion had disturbed the town, wondered Lily? Had the blacksmith, Art Kinley, stirred in his cot far side of the forge? Was he pulling on his pants even now, blinking his eyes clear of sleep to go take a look at the mounts?

Lily could see the indecision on Prince's face as he continued to wait and watch and listen. Maybe it was time to back off, leave the matter a while. After, all, nobody was going nowhere, were they, except on his say-so?

No saying what it was that decided Prince to move when he did, take the two steps from where he had halted and come face on to the shadows.

Lily had already gasped and put a hand to her mouth a moment before the single shot roared across the icy morning, spinning Prince's Colt from his grip in a spurt of blood that showered like crimson snow to the dirt.

Seconds later there was only the uneasy silence and neither sight nor sound of the drifter. And the shadows then were truly empty.

Fifteen

It took Lily a half-hour of constant shouting and banging on the bedroom door before Jonas Bantry, his face wet with sweat, eyes red-rimmed, shirt stretched to near bursting across his paunch, finally arrived with the key and set her free.

'Against my personal better judgement, but Tove says to turn yuh loose again,' he sneered, watching from the open door as Lily gathered her shawl and flung it across her shoulders. 'Seems like Mr Prince won't be needin' yuh for a while.'

'You bet he won't!' smiled Lily. 'I seen it all from up here. Know somethin', Jonas, I figure for yuh havin' a whole heap of trouble pilin' up with whoever it is callin' the shots out there. The drifter still about?'

' 'Course he ain't,' snapped Jonas, wiping a hand over his face. 'Long gone, I shouldn't wonder.'

'But he'll be back again, and that's what's botherin' yuh, ain't it? And yuh won't know when, and yuh won't know where.'

'Yuh know somethin' about this drifter?' said Bantry, his eyes narrowing.

'No more than you,' said Lily. 'Just drifted in, didn't he? Joe Blossom's belt along of him. Bad news, Jonas, bad news.' She moved closer to him, her gaze fixed on his watery stare. 'Goin' to need the fella out of the way before that stage rolls in, aren't yuh? So how yuh goin' to do that? How long yuh got? How long's the man goin' to give yuh?'

Bantry sneered menacingly. 'Keep yuh thoughts to yourself, Lily. And just remember, you and me ain't through yet. I owe yuh some for this lump back of my head. Best be askin' yourself how long yuh figure you've got.'

The sun had long cleared the peaks, burned off the frost and lifted the first shadows to noon, when the funeral procession finally got under way and the wagons and followers began their slow steps and trundle through the town to Boot Hill.

The mood was sad and mournful enough, but not without a spark of some curiosity among those who had paid close attention to the shooting back of the livery.

'What's happenin', Doc?' Elias Macks had asked when the first opportunity had presented itself. 'Rumour has it that Prince is hit. That a fact? Is that drifter back in town? Yuh want for me to try rousin' some of the boys? Hell, Doc, just what in the name of sanity is goin' on around here?'

Doc's answers had been brief and guarded.

Yes, Prince had been hit; treated the wound himself not two hours back; one of his gun hands out of action and likely to be so for some time. Who had done the shooting? Well, yes, very likely it had been the drifting man. But no one had seen him. Hell, no, Macks was not to go rousing anybody. Was there anybody fit enough to be roused?

As for what the hell was going on – 'You tell me, Elias. You tell me.'

But Macks had not been for giving up quite so easily. 'Somethin's brewing,' he had murmured, walking at Doc's side. 'You can smell somethin's brewing. Tove's into no good. Got to be. Somethin' big – big enough to kill Joe Blossom for. But what? Yuh ain't seen that drifter, have yuh, Doc?'

' 'Course not,' Doc had lied and looked away quickly. No point in saying the fellow had stood in his front parlour and talked with him for over an hour, was there? What good would it do? Best leave it for now. See how things panned out.

It was long after noon when the dead had finally been laid to rest, the last words spoken, the last hymn sung. Doc led the mourners silently back to town and told them all to go home, tend to the living, do the best they could to look to the future, wherever they might find it.

Doc, for his part, had other matters to attend.

Cornelius Tove helped himself to his third large whiskey, swigged a half of it and stared long and hard at

Boden Prince seated alone at a table on the far side of the otherwise deserted saloon bar.

Fellow was struggling some, he thought. Not so much the pain in his hand that was troubling him as the dent his pride had taken. How long since anybody had got the better of Boden Prince when it came to trading lead? If the fellow doing the shooting from the shadows had had the time and skill to select his target, and take out one of Prince's hands, how come he had left him standing? He could have finished it then and there.

More to the point, Prince knew it. Knew too the fellow would be back to do just that.

What, of course, he did not know – what none of them knew – was who the drifter really was. And what manner of game was he playing now? He could not possibly know of Tove's plans for the stage when it arrived in Wargrit, so what did he have to gain by risking his own skin in coming back when a clear trail into the Crowfoots had beckoned?

And how come nobody had seen the drifter make his return? Somebody must have. . . .

'T'ain't no use dwellin' on what's happened,' murmured Pitch at Tove's side, his back to Prince. 'He ain't goin' to be a deal of use for a while. We need to make some plans.'

'Such as?'

'Such as, gettin' ourselves another gun.'

'That goin' to be necessary?'

'Very. Yuh seen what that drifter can do, and don't

tell me yuh ain't lookin' to him bein' back. He'll be
here, just when it suits.'

Tove grunted and swigged at the whiskey. 'So what
do yuh figure?'

'I suggest we put it to Prince that we need another
gun out of San Apee. He'll see the sense in that and
know who to recruit and where we'll find him. Then we
send Jonas to go fetch him. Pronto. Like now. Agreed?'

'Don't seem like we have a choice.'

'We don't, not if we're still goin' ahead with what we
planned. And to do that we *need* another gun – and that
drifter dead.'

'Both,' murmured Tove.

'Both. No messin'. Soon as we can.'

Tove finished his whiskey in a single gulp.

Jonas Bantry could think of a dozen better ways of
spending his time than riding hard for San Apee. He
could be looking to the stocktaking at his mercantile —
no mean task if you wanted the fine edge on the best
profit – or he could be putting his feet up with a good
whiskey to hand and a quality cigar at his lips. He could
just as easily be teaching that whore, Lily Hassels, a
sharp lesson in decent, ladylike behaviour, and enjoy-
ing every minute of it.

But no, he was here, late afternoon on the fast trail
out of Wargrit heading directly and at some lick, for a
meeting with one Clem McCourt, at the Silver Palace
hotel in San Apee. McCourt would hear him out with
his message from Boden Prince and in no time at all

have a half-dozen top-rate hired guns kicking dust on their way to join Prince and Cornelius Tove in Wargrit.

No problem, no sweat.

Not quite to plan, of course, thought Bantry, swallowing on an already parched throat as his mount raced on through the gathering sweep of early dusk shadows. No one had bargained for the drifter coming back to town; no one could see any good reason why he should, but the fact was he was there, or thereabouts, and somebody had somehow to deal with him and keep the lid on folk getting any fancy ideas that with Prince wounded they might come to squaring up to Tove again. Wargrit had to stay quiet, at least until the rerouted stage out of Springfield pulled in. And if the price of a quiet town was some spitting of fast lead from guns with no edge to argue either way, so be it.

Another few days and the place would be a memory anyhow.

Jonas settled to the hard riding, his thoughts already drifting to the golden days to come when he would be king of the mercantile tycoons with Bantry's stores stretching nationwide, coast to coast, once the Oregon trails were opened up and the big drive West got underway.

Yessir, coast to coast. . . .

He was still a handful of miles short of the outskirts of San Apee when the rider, tall in the saddle, riding easy, hands loose to relaxed reins, broke across the trail in the shadows way ahead of him. No saying at this distance who the fellow was, where exactly he had come from, but there was no doubting what he had in mind. Jonas had no choice. The long-barrelled Colt in the fellow's grip was doing all the talking necessary.

Sixteen

'Nasty,' said Doc, peeling the bloodstained bandage from Boden Prince's hand. 'Yuh should quit meddlin' with guns!'

Prince snarled and hissed through his stained teeth. 'Don't get smart. I shoot just as well with the good hand.'

'I'm sure yuh do,' murmured Doc, squinting for a closer look at the wound. 'Just as well in your line of business. Be a while before yuh get to fillin' this one with a gun.'

'Just do the dressin',' growled Prince. 'Yuh ain't paid for the advice.'

Doc shrugged and bent to his task, conscious of Tove hovering at his back. 'Yuh see anythin' of that drifter, Doc?' he asked, almost absently. 'Sure comes and goes awful quiet.'

'Not me,' grunted Doc. 'I ain't had a deal of time for socializin' or payin' heed to folk, save to bind 'em up or lay 'em out. Yuh must've noticed!'

Prince winced. Tove moved beyond Doc to the bar in the deserted, shadow-lined saloon. 'Fella's gettin'to be a real nuisance.' He adjusted the bandage at his shoulder and dusted a speck of dirt from the lapel of his coat. 'Still,' he added with a soft grin, 'it's of no consequence. We'll soon have the matter sorted.'

Doc grunted again, finished treating Prince's hand, slid the roll of dressings to his bag and reached for his hat. 'Yuh got any more wounded?' he mouthed cynically. 'Likely to have? Or are yuh waitin' on Bantry's return?'

'Don't miss much for a busy man, do yuh?' sneered Tove. 'What else ain't yuh missed?'

'Too damned much,' snapped Doc. 'Biggest miss bein' why we're goin' through all this. What's the deal, Tove? What yuh hatchin' here like some slink-eyed rattler?'

Pitch coughed lightly from a corner table. 'Tell him. What we got to lose? Could come in useful if things get awkward. We might need a doc.'

Tove thought for a moment, murmured to himself, then turned slowly to face Doc. 'Why not?' he grinned. 'San Apee stage out of Springfield is schedulin' a stop right here, in Wargrit. Four passengers on board. We're only interested in one.'

'A passenger?' frowned Doc.

'A certain Miss Caitlin Paterson, only daughter of Spencer J. Paterson, president of the North County Bank and sundry other companies and organizations. A man of some considerable property and means.'

'Considerable,' echoed Pitch.

'Miss Paterson is travelling to join her pa in San Apee under the escort of one of Paterson's personal body-guards. Wargrit is as far as she goes.'

Doc swallowed. 'Yuh plan on kidnappin' her. That it? Yuh goin' to hold her to ransom?'

'S'right,' smiled Tove benevolently.

'But how—?'

'That's enough, Doc,' called Pitch from the corner. 'Yuh heard all yuh need to hear for now. The rest yuh'll likely as not witness – if yuh stay lucky.'

'Yuh'll never get away with it,' said Doc, tightening his grip on his bag. 'Yuh playin' big stakes here, Tove. Too big even for the likes of you. Why, I shouldn't won-der if that Paterson fella don't—'

'Shut it, Doc,' flared Tove. 'I don't want to hear no more from you. You wanna stay healthy, you just—'

The batwings crashed open and a youth, wide-eyed, sweat gleaming like steam on his face, his lips twitching nervously, a Winchester fixed and heavy in his grip, strad-dled the space, the wings creaking eerily behind him.

'Yuh killed my pa,' he croaked. 'Right there in the street. Him, that scumbag.' He gestured the rifle at Prince. 'Time's come for a reckonin'.'

Young Jamie Cain, thought Doc, releasing the grip on his bag, not yet seventeen and as short-sighted as a liquored gopher.

'Now!' groaned the youth.

'Hold it!' shouted Doc, stepping between the youth and Prince. 'Hold it right there, Jamie. This ain't no way to

106

settle things.'

'An eye for an eye like the Good Book says,' flared
Cain, still sweating.

'Ain't arguin' with the Book,' said Doc, 'but there's
been enough blood spilled in this town. Let's calm it,
eh? And yuh pa wouldn't go thankin' you for no hot
head fool's work, Jamie, so yuh put aside that piece and
get y'self back to yuh ma. All right?'

'Yuh stand clear, Doc,' shuddered Jamie, tightening
his grip. 'I ain't for doin' you no harm, but I swear I'll
shoot straight through yuh if yuh don't shift.'

'Sure yuh will, and yuh would too. Don't doubt yuh,
son, but like I say we seen enough blood spilled lately
and I ain't for moppin' up no more of it.' Doc smiled
softly and eased a step closer to the youth. 'Yuh'll get
yuh day, boy, rest assured, so don't yuh go spoilin'
nothin' for y'self. Damnit, Jamie, town needs every able-
bodied to stand to it 'til we're through with this. Don't
you go lettin' nobody down now, specially yuh kin and
me.'

Jamie Cain stared hard at Doc, at Prince where the
gunslinger nursed his wounded hand, at Tove, then at
Doc again. 'I just wanted . . .' he began.

'Sure,' soothed Doc, easing the Winchester from
Jamie's hands. 'Know just how yuh feel, son. And yuh
ain't the only one.'

'Get him outa here,' sneered Tove. 'And don't let me
see no more heroes steppin' through them 'wings. Next
one as does gets carried out!'

Doc collected his bag, glared at Tove, and led the

youth silently from the bar back to the night and the dimly lit street.

'Could've got y'self shot through there, yuh realize that?' snapped Doc when they reached the boardwalk. 'Darn fool thing to go doin'. All it needed—'

'I know, I know,' murmured Jamie, glancing back to the bar, 'but Lily said as how it was the only way to get yuh outa there without Tove nosyin' after yuh.'

'Lily?' frowned Doc.

'She sent me. Said as how yuh were to come to her fast. Your place. Right now, Doc.'

'What the hell's goin' on, f'Cris'sake?'

'It's the driftin' fella,' whispered Jamie, hurrying Doc into the shadows. 'He's showed up again. Not an hour ago.'

'Where?' hissed Doc.

'Your back porch, Doc. Large as life. Jonas Bantry trussed and gagged along of him.'

'Bantry? But how—?'

'Lily was already there, waitin' on yuh. They sent me to the bar to get yuh.'

'Right, right,' said Doc, quickening his step. 'Now if yuh wanna do somethin' really useful in the name of your pa, son, yuh get y'self settled some place where yuh can watch every move them rats back there get to makin'. And yuh let me know minute they do. Yuh got it, Jamie?'

'Got it,' smiled the youth.

Doc patted his shoulder and was gone before Jamie had time to blink.

Tove stood to the side of the batwings and waited for the shapes deep in the darkness of the night to begin to move. Or would they, he wondered? Maybe not. Maybe there was nothing out there to move. Could be he had done exactly what he had threatened and silenced the town of Wargrit until nothing and nobody shifted except on his say so.

Just as it should be – for now. But he would feel a whole sight more comfortable with some reliable guns a shade closer to hand.

'How long before we see your boys?' he asked, without turning to Prince.

'Sun-up,' muttered the gunslinger from a table by the bar.

Tove nodded and checked his timepiece. 'We shall need everythin' in position by midday tomorrow. Ain't no sayin' as to the exact time the stage'll hit town, but I'd reckon late afternoon. What yuh say, Marcus? That your reckonin'?'

'Sounds about right,' clipped the gambler from the shadowed corner.

'How good's your good hand goin' to be, Prince?'

'Good enough. Yuh'll have no cause for complaint.'

'I hope not,' grinned Tove. 'I want the killin' done with quickly, and not a hair on the Paterson girl's head so much as ruffled. That clear?'

'Clear,' grunted Prince, his gaze emptying on the night beyond the pale glow of the bar's lantern light.

'Do we need Bantry?' asked Pitch, dealing the cards across a game of Patience.

'Do we?' repeated Tove, staring into the street.

'Served his purpose, ain't he? Tends to get nervy. Tongue happy too on occasions.'

'Same as Joe Blossom,' murmured Tove.

'Exactly the same as Joe.'

The men were silent for a moment.

'So we kill him,' said Pitch at last.

'Mr Prince'll see to it,' answered Tove.

The gunslinger's gaze stayed unblinking.

The men were silent again for a while.

'Town's quiet,' said Pitch.

Cornelius Tove was tempted to add 'as the grave', but thought better of it and said nothing.

'Yeah,' drawled Prince, coming to his feet and crossing to the 'wings. 'As the grave,' he added to Tove's annoyance and irritable sidelong glance.

Why tempt fate, wondered Pitch?

Seventeen

Doc Brands squinted through the shadowy gloom of his front parlour at the bulk of Jonas Bantry roped to a chair in the darkest corner of the room, and chuckled softly to himself. 'Never thought I'd see the day. Nossiree! Real sight for sore eyes, ain't he?'

Lily Hassels folded her arms defiantly across her breasts and slid her weight to one hip. 'Say that again,' she smiled, 'but what in hell we goin' to do with him?'

'Wouldn't have a notion right now,' chuckled Doc again. 'Ain't fussed none neither. He can wait. Tell me about the drifter. Where's he headed? Did he say? What's he plannin', and did he say anythin' about—?'

'Hold up there,' said Lily. 'Didn't say a lot – just delivered that old fossil and said as how he was ridin' out to meet the stage at Doon Drift.'

'The stage . . .' mused Doc. 'I told him about that, but he can't know about the Paterson girl, not unless. . . . 'Course, he mebbe got it out of Bantry. So. . . .' he pondered.

111

'I ain't got a clue what the fella's plannin', Doc, and I don't see we're servin' any good on tryin' to reckon it. Seems to me we got to figure how best to stay alive between now and Tove gettin' his hands on that stage. He does that, and we're corralled.'

Doc thudded his hands to a tight clasp behind his back and paced the length of the room. 'Bantry must have been headin' for San Apee to raise new guns. Well, that's one thing ain't goin' to happen. The drifter's headed out to meet the stage. So what's he goin' to do – slow it down, halt it, reroute it? We ain't goin' to know 'til it happens. Meantime. . . .'

'Meantime,' said Lily, 'Tove's goin' to be gettin' hot under the collar, and I wouldn't give two-bits for how he might spill over once he figures there ain't goin' to be no new guns, and that the driftin' fella's shown up again.'

'We get ourselves a step ahead,' clipped Doc suddenly. 'We got Bantry, we know about the stage, we know where the drifters headed – we got an edge here, Lil. We'd best use it.'

'Glad you can see it. Don't look to be much from where I'm standin'.'

'Well, mebbe not,' smiled Doc, 'but it's there. Now. . . . You get y'self back to the saloon. We need eyes there, Lil, and you're goin' to be them. I'll be in touch.' He consulted the clock on the wall. 'Time to talk to some of the boys,' he murmured.

'Just hope you know what yuh doin' here, Doc,' frowned Lily.

'No,' said Doc, 'can't rightly say I do. But it's the best I can see for us right now, so I guess we're just goin' to have to give it our best shot. What yuh say?'

Lily simply smiled and nodded, her head already reeling.

Boden Prince had never been one for a deal of sleep. It could be a dangerous, not to say fatal, luxury for a fella who made his living by the Colt and walked forever in the shadows of his enemies. You get to too much sleeping, and the shadows get to reaching.

No problem, therefore, when it came to Tove and Pitch turning in and leaving their trusted, albeit wounded, gunslinger to stand watch. Prince would doze and cat-nap when he felt it safe to do so. But this, he had decided early on, was definitely not the night for it.

There was too much happening, or perhaps not enough, he thought, watching the town's main street from the shadowed boardwalk at the Best Bet saloon. Place seemed quiet enough, sure it did; almost total darkness, not so much as the flicker of a late night light, and not the whisper of a sound, not even from a scavenging hound or a restless mount at the livery.

Everybody tucked up and sleeping peaceful, he wondered, or were there some with one eye open, some still fully clothed with their boots on their feet and their gunbelts ready strapped? You never could tell when a town had been pushed this far.

But Boden Prince's aversion to sleep on this night was not entirely his natural regard and respect for the hours of darkness and what they might hold.

Tonight he was still pondering the mysterious drifter and how it was the fellow had taken him out so neatly back of the livery. How come, damnit, he had left him standing when it would have been a whole lot easier to kill him?

And there was too the no less pressing question of just where the fellow was now, if he was here at all.

'Hmmm,' he murmured quietly to himself, the good hand lifted to rub across his stubbled chin; the sooner the fresh guns out of San Apee arrived the better. He just hoped Bantry had ridden hard and fast and got to the business matters before straying to the waiting bar girls at the Silver Palace.

He eased himself from the deepest of the shadows and strolled softly across the boardwalk, passing the glow of pale light at the bar's window, the dark shapes beyond the batwings, and paused at the few steps from the boards to the dirt street. Still no sounds, still nothing moving.

He had half-turned as if to move back to the 'wings when he heard the creak. Somebody moving; not close; far side of the street; Bantry's mercantile. Prince's eyes narrowed as he peered closer, probing the dark sprawl of the store. Nothing.

He waited. Another creak, this time to the left, heading away from the store. His gaze shifted quickly. There – narrow alley between the mercantile and a rundown storage. Might have been a body, thought Prince, somebody in a hurry not to be seen, moving to the rear of Bantry's place.

He fingered the butt of his holstered Colt with his good hand, felt for the steps from the boards to the street without shifting his gaze and moved towards the store. Could be some smart fella had figured for Bantry being out of town and reckoned on helping himself from a sleeping store. Too bad. He was going to be out of luck!

Prince had paused again, this time to listen for what he was now certain would be the squeak of a door when the batwings at his back creaked on their parched hinges.

He swung round, the Colt fixed in his grip, eyes narrowed on the bar's shadowed boardwalk. 'Who the—' he began, then relaxed, the gun looser in his grip, his gaze a touch brighter.

'Can't yuh sleep?' pouted Lily, one hand on the half-open 'wings. She grinned. 'Get to hearin' things this time of night, don't yuh? Who yuh hearin' Mr Prince? Yuh got some ghosts driftin' round yuh there?'

Prince took a last look at the store, holstered the Colt and stepped back to the boards.

'Might ask the same of you,' he grunted, closing on the batwings.

'Share a drink on it, shall we?' said Lily, her gaze flicking quickly to the dark, deserted store, her smile, she thought, just warm enough to draw Prince's attention from the sudden shift of shadows at the back of him.

But it had been close.

'Well?' hissed Doc, ushering Jamie Cain to the depths of his kitchen and closing the door gently behind him. 'What's the picture?'

'Pretty much as we thought, Doc,' said the youth, wiping a sliver of sweat from his brow. 'Just Prince around at the moment. Looks as if Tove and Pitch are sleepin' back of the bar. But Miss Lily's got to the gunslinger, sharp as a rattler spittin' venom. He didn't see nothin' of me.'

'Yuh got to the store?' asked Doc.

'Sure. Got right in. Back door. Do it again anytime yuh like.'

'Good,' smiled Doc, rubbing his hands. 'Next thing is to get to Elias. Yuh reckon yuh can do that, Jamie? Go wake Macks and bring him here? Not a sound. Yuh manage that?'

'Sure thing, Doc. Get to it right now.' Jamie peered through the open door to the parlour where the trussed bulk of Bantry slumped on the chair in the corner. 'What we goin' to do with him, Doc? Deserves to hang, don't he? He's been in with them scum since the start of it.'

'Too right he has,' said Doc. 'But don't you get to frettin' on his fate, Jamie. Mr Bantry here ain't goin' to get away with nothin'. Yuh got my word on it. Now, yuh goin' to get to Macks. . . .'

'Well, now, Jonas,' smiled Doc to the trussed, gagged, toad-eyed bulk when Jamie had left the room, 'seems like I might have to get to protectin' yuh from a lynch mob, don't it?'

Bantry moaned. His eyes rolled.

'Turn yuh loose on the town now and I reckon they'd be for tearin' yuh to pieces. Figure yuh could count on yuh compatriots then, do yuh? I reckon not, Jonas. Know what – I'd wager for them not givin' a damn for yuh, 'specially when they get to realizin' yuh never made it to San Apee for them fresh guns.'

Doc smiled and settled his hands tight behind him. 'Looks like bein' one helluva day comin' up, don't it? Yessir, one helluva day!'

Eighteen

For a town seemingly dead to the world in its deep if troubled slumbers through the long night hours, Wargrit was a busy place. Shapes flitted silently, briefly through the shadows like ghosts; they came and went from corner to corner, door to door, window to window in a steady stream of activity as news went the rounds that Bantry was being held at Doc's home, the drifting man had been in town and left again, that a stage was coming in, that something was being planned. . . .

Elias Macks, still nursing the dull throb of his wound, had wasted no time in responding to Doc's call. 'We goin' to make a stand of it?' he had croaked, slipping into Doc's darkened kitchen.

'Hell, no,' Doc had said, closing the door behind him. 'Had enough of that, ain't we?'

'But with Prince hit like he is—'

'Yeah, yeah,' Doc had soothed. 'I hear yuh thinkin', but I ain't for losin' any more lives, not if there's the spit of a chance of doin' things another way.'

'I'm listenin'.'

'Way I see it,' Doc had begun, and in the next half-hour had outlined his sketchy plan to a concentrating Macks. 'Best we can do, leastways 'til we see how things pan out,' he had concluded.

'Count me in,' Macks had grinned. 'I'll get the news out straight away. You can handle Bantry here?'

'Oh, sure, me and Jonas are gettin' along just fine. He ain't no trouble!'

For all that they had suffered at the hands of Tove and his sidekicks, and in spite of many still nursing their grief and loss, there was no shortage of offers to lend a hand wherever it might be needed.

'Tell Doc, he's only got to say the word. We'll be there,' had been the consensus, so that long before the first light had blinked in the east, and with the night frost sharp as glass where it had gripped, the town, it seemed, was ready – quite for what it did not fully understand. Point was, Wargrit and its folk would still be standing come the end of the day. And that, for now, was resolve enough.

There were still shapes among and between the shadows long after Doc finally got to dozing at the kitchen table.

Boden Prince had not slept a wink, barely closed his eyes, come to that, as Lily Hassels could vouch for. She had watched him for what now seemed hours; the slow pacing of the bar to the batwings, pausing, watching, listening; pacing back again, his stare thoughtful,

somewhere else – and certainly not on her, Lily had
noted thankfully – another turn, another measured
walk to the 'wings, a longer, deeper probing of the
empty street as if expecting somebody, or something,
to be there.

He was getting suspicious, thought Lily. Maybe he
figured for the fresh guns from San Apee being here by
now. Maybe he was wondering if Bantry had turned
turkey and kept riding, too spooked to see things
through. Or had he fouled up right there in the Silver
Palace? Hell, he should have been the one to ride.

Or maybe he was thinking about the drifter, wondering if and when he might be back again. Wondering if
next time things might be a whole lot different.

Perhaps they would, Lily had mused, in her half-
asleep state. She had seen the man, been in his company, for less than an hour; exchanged no more than a
half-dozen words with him, watched him ride out, heading for Doon Drift. Just a shape in the night.

But he would be back. She knew it. Prince knew it.

The sound of hurrying steps. Somebody heading this
way, and in no mood for showing any respect to those
still sleeping.

'Just what in hell's name's goin' on in this town?' Art
Kinley, from the livery, pounding down the street to the
bar, arms waving, voice croaking and cracking over his
words. 'Some goddamn, half-crazed sonofabitch's gone
and turned the horses loose! Livery's empty. There ain't
a mount in town, f'Cris'sake!'

Art had thudded to the 'wings and crashed them

open almost before Prince had turned from pouring himself a stiff drink.

'Yuh hear what I'm sayin', mister?' ranted Art. 'I been robbed! Horses have gone – includin' yours! Don't tell me this is another piece of Tove's doin', 'cos if it is—'

The private back room door opened on Marcus Pitch struggling into his jacket, his face wet with the sweat of sleep.

'Yuh hear that?' snapped Prince, turning to the gambler. 'Somebody's hit the livery.'

'Who?' groaned Pitch, blinking on the pale light. 'Who'd wanna do that?'

'Who do yuh think?' said Prince.

Pitched blinked, shook his senses into focus and stared at Art. 'Yuh saw nothin', heard nothin'?'

' 'Course I didn't. Think I'd be standin' here if I had? Goddamnit, do yuh realize what this means? Means we ain't got four legs would carry a body as far as the Crowfoots. Better ask Mr Tove just what he's plannin' to do about that, hadn't yuh?'

Cornelius Tove was in no mood for being asked so much as the time of day when he finally emerged from the back room, his crumpled jacket and trousers clear evidence of a restless night.

'Get me some coffee,' he had snapped at Lily. Then, turning to Pitch, 'What the hell's goin' on?' And, turning again, this time to glare at Prince. 'Where's them guns? Do somethin', damnit!'

Art Kinley had continued to rant, stomp around the

bar and shout his abuse at whoever, and sometimes whatever, came into view. 'I'm lookin' at my whole liveli-hood disappearin' here, yuh understand that? Any of yuh? Hell, if a livery and stables ain't got horses, what in tarnation is a fella supposed to be doin', f'Cris'sake? Answer me that, will yuh?'

'Shut him up,' Tove had ordered, glancing at Prince.

'Shootin' ain't solvin' nothin',' Pitch had inter-rupted, draining the dregs of a whiskey bottle.

'What yuh sayin'?' Tove had glowered.

'I'm sayin' as how it's obvious what's goin' on, ain't it? Plain as the nose on yuh face. That driftin' fella's back in town – and he's keepin' busy.'

'Then get him, for God's sake!'

Prince's good hand slid to the butt of his Colt.

'Hold it,' said Pitch. 'Pointless just steppin' out there, ain't it? Yuh don't figure for the fella waitin' on yuh, surely? 'Course he ain't. He can bide his time for as long as he chooses. What we need is Bantry with them San Apee guns.' He glanced at the bar clock. 'How much longer do yuh reckon?'

Prince shrugged. 'All depends on the storekeeper, don't it?' he drawled. 'If he got himself fazed out with them Palace gals. . . . Well, no sayin'.'

'If he's done that—' began Tove, but swung round, the words lost, as the batwings creaked and a dusty-faced, down-at-heel youth in patched pants held at his waist on a length of knotted twine stepped into the bar and laid Jonas Bantry's hat carefully on the table near-est to him.

122

'Where'd yuh get that?' croaked Tove, his face draining of what little colour it had mustered.

'Out . . . out there . . . on the boardwalk,' stammered the youth, blinking wildly. 'Front of Mr . . . Mr Bantry's store. Whole heap of his clothes, all of 'em, right down to his johns and that.' He swallowed. 'But he ain't in 'em, Mr Tove. There ain't a hint of him.'

Tove had abandoned the pot of fresh coffee and opened a bottle of whiskey. Prince had already helped himself to his own bottle. Pitch had lit a fat cigar and left the bar for the keener, cleaner air of the boardwalk. Art Kinley was at the centre of a gathering of men in the street, their voices low and careful, their glances at Pitch, the saloon, Bantry's mercantile, furtive and anxious. The light was thin and still struggling to clear the high peaks, the air ice-edged and frosty, but nobody seemed to feel the chill. It was getting to be natural in Wargrit.

'Well,' said Prince, easing to Pitch's side, 'yuh want for me to get busy?'

Pitch grunted and stared at the gunslinger's bandaged hand. 'Pushin' the odds somewhat, aren't we?'

'One shot's as good as two if it hits the target.'

'Yuh reckon yuh can find that drifter?'

'I can if he's here,' grinned Prince. 'Or are yuh pullin' out?'

'Bantry ain't no big loss,' said Pitch, flicking cigar ash to the dirt.

'Yuh for cuttin' me in on this deal?'

123

'Do I have a choice?'

Prince's fingers danced on the butt of his Colt. 'None,' he smiled, 'not if yuh stickin' to yuh plan. Yuh goin' to need me. A mite short on guns, aren't yuh? Horses too. And just what's happened to Bantry? Is he here? Out there on the trail? Never made it to San Apee, that's for sure. So, all things considered—'

'Sure, yuh made yuh point,' said Pitch. 'Count y'self in, but, let's not get to wastin' too much time, eh? Stage will be here this afternoon. That part of the operation's got to go without a hitch. Minute that Paterson gal steps down to the boardwalk. . . . Like I say, let's not waste our time.'

Prince grunted, his fingers still dancing on the gun butt. 'You just keep this town off my back, all right? 'Specially that meddlin' doc and his cronies. And another thing,' he grinned, moving to the steps to the street, 'yuh keep that woman, Lily Hassels, warm for me. She comes with the deal.'

Pitch concentrated on his cigar and the smoke that curled from it; here one minute, gone the next.

Nineteen

'Prince's on the move,' hissed Jamie Cain, sidling into Doc's kitchen. 'Just left the saloon, lookin' mean as a rat for all he's only got one hand. Do we leave him?'

'Let him prowl,' said Doc. 'He ain't goin' to find nothin'. Drifter's somewhere out of town, and Bantry's in my loft. Pitch and Tove still in the bar?'

'Ain't shifted. Don't look as if they're plannin' to neither. Still smartin' like they had fleas over Bantry.' Jamie tittered quietly. 'Can't figure, can they, how the storekeeper's clothes got where we left 'em? And they ain't a notion where he is right now.'

'Probably ain't a deal bothered,' grunted Doc. 'Mebbe more concerned about the lack of horses.'

'Yeah,' smiled Jamie. 'Art played that real well, eh? Snaffled his horses out to the old Packet homestead and then swore large as life as how he'd been robbed. They believed him too!'

'Hmmm,' pondered Doc, 'but for how long? We gotta keep things movin' along 'til that stage pulls in.'

'And then what?' frowned Jamie.

'Good question, son, good question.' Doc scratched his chin and adjusted the spectacles on the tip of his nose. 'And yuh know somethin' – I just don't have the snitch of an answer.'

It took Boden Prince less than an hour to conclude that the drifter had at some time, by some means, hightailed it out of town. There was no chance he was still in Wargrit; no chance that somebody was keeping him hidden back of a woodshed, in a spare room, under the floorboards or some such place. The fellow had ridden out. And that, to Prince's reckoning, was a whole sight worse than having him skulking through the street shadows.

'Put him where I can see him,' he had complained to Pitch, between generous measures of whiskey, 'and I can handle the sonofabitch. But this way, when he could be anywhere 'tween here and the Crowfoots, and that's another thing.'

'Yuh wanna go chasin' him?' Pitch had asked. 'Assumin' yuh can find a horse.'

'No I guess not. I ain't takin' my eye off that stage.'

'I figured not,' smiled Pitch. 'So we wait, eh? Another hour, two at most. Relax. Still got the edge here, ain't we?'

Prince had simply poured another whiskey.

Lily Hassels was in no mood to compromise. Another few hours and she would be free, putting Wargrit, the sights and smells of it, behind her and heading out, trailing to any place she chose just as long as it put miles between her and the prospect of more of the likes of Tove, Pitch, Bantry and that scumbag, Prince.

Minute that stage pulled in and Tove got to settling whatever he had in mind, she would be gone, slipping away in the confusion to the livery where Art Kinley had promised on his life to have a horse waiting for her, and then riding like the wind north, south, who cared? And if there were any of the bar girls, or anybody else come to that, with similar intent, they were welcome to join her. Bring your own mount!

She sighed, stared at the bedroll tied neat and tight on the chair in her room, and reflected for a moment that it and the clothes she stood in were just about all she had to show for her years in Wargrit. But, then, maybe she was lucky to be getting out with her life – if she did.

Pity she could not persuade Doc to ride with her, but, like he had said, 'Yuh get to my age, and the grass don't look nothin' like so green far side of the hill. Grass stays grass most places.'

She sighed again and turned to the window. Street below was empty, town quiet. Even Tove had calmed himself. Pitch and Prince would be huddled in deep talk, and Jonas Bantry – she smiled – well, now, seemed like Jonas had stepped out of his pants once too often!

The smile faded. Shame she had not held on to the storekeeper's shotgun. She was maybe going to need it.

*

The sun climbed high and the day grew warmer, the shadows thicker and the light sharper and keener through the late Fall air.

Noon came and went. The street stayed empty, the boardwalks quiet. Even the town drunk stayed home and dried out.

Art Kinley retired to his livery and busied himself convincingly around the deserted stables. Miras Carter worked systematically, if at times feverishly, in the preparation of more coffins. Pine planking was now at a premium.

Doc Brands paced the length of his front parlour and back again, pausing every few minutes to check his bag, turn to the window in expectation of Jamie's wave to say the stage was rolling in, and then on again as the minutes ticked by and another hour passed.

Elias Macks and a group of the town men waited patiently back of the one-time saddlery, their conversation light and casual, their senses fine-tuned for the only sound they wanted to hear – the beat of hoofs, creak and grind of stage timbers, snap of leather, echoing jangle of tack, call of the driver to the straining team as the town hoved into view. Some of the men were chilled. Others sweated.

Lily Hassels stared from the window of her room and wondered what sort of view she would have from the next window in whatever new town she drifted into. Two bits to nothing it would be a street.

Cornelius Tove plucked grey hairs from his side-burns. Marcus Pitch played a bad hand of Patience. Boden Prince flexed anxious fingers over the butt of his holstered Colt.

Somewhere an old-timer played out a mournful tune on an ancient harmonica. Nobody seemed to mind.

Doc Brands' front parlour clock showed three-twenty-six when Jamie Cain waved excitedly to him from the boardwalk.

The stage was on its way.

It came out of the blood-red glow of the already sinking sun like the shafted bulk of a foreboding shadow: a dark, silhouetted shape, the horses straining and heaving to the pace, eyes white-rimmed and wild, manes and tails flying to the dust cloud swirling in a yellow mist.

The voice of the weatherbeaten, barrel-chested driver, one Tubs Casey, a long-time employee of the Springfield Stage Line, rose on the late afternoon air like the calling of some crazed bird of prey, the words indecipherable, the sounds twitching the ears of the team as they responded without effort to the driver's every command and flick of the reins.

Seated at Tubs' side was his trusted friend and working companion – 'Slickest shotgun this side of the Crowfoots' – Charlie Weeld.

Tubs and Charlie had been teamed driver and shotgun on the Springfield–San Apee run for the past five years. They knew their teams, the trail, the whims and fancies of the territorial weather better than they knew themselves, save for this occasion on this day following the rerouted trail via Doon Drift and Wargrit.

Neither man had set eyes on the town in a good many years. Neither would have bothered now given the choice. But there had been no choice. The man at the Drift had made that perfectly clear.

'Town's comin' up!' yelled Charlie, above the creaks and squeaks, grating of wheels to axles, thud of hoofs, snap of leather and tack. 'Don't see no welcomin' party.'

'Don't worry,' shouted Tubs. 'They'll be there.'

The stage swayed on, the dust cloud swirling behind it to shroud the backdrop of the Crowfoot mountains.

Charlie took a moment to ease aside the Winchester cradled in his lap and consult his timepiece. 'Right on time,' he called to his companion.

Tubs Casey yelled something only his horses seemed to understand.

'No shootin' until it's necessary,' hissed Tove from the deepest shadows of the boardwalk flanking the batwings. 'And for God's sake mind the girl. She ain't worth a spit dead.'

'What yuh goin' to do with her once she's taken?' asked Prince, watching the approaching dust cloud.

'Don't fret,' sneered Tove. 'Yuh can leave that side of things to me.'

'Sure,' said Prince. 'Just don't f'get I got a cut in this deal. Yuh look to my share real good, eh?'

Tove grunted sardonically and turned his stare to the

trail and the rolling sway of the stage. 'Been a while, eh, Marcus?' he murmured, glancing at Pitch. 'Sometimes wondered if we'd ever get to it. But – damn it, here we are. Just a few more turns of them wheels, coupla hours or so to get organized, two days for the deal to come through and . . . presto, we made it! Still plannin' on California?'

'I ain't plannin' no further than this stage pullin' in and that gal steppin' down to the boards here. That's the sum total of my plannin'.'

Tove simply smiled and fingered the curls of his side-burns.

Elias Macks and the town men moved nervously from their cover at the saddlery to the main street, conscious of the grief and disaster that had followed in the wake of the last time they stepped up to the Best Bet saloon.

A handful of curious wives, young girls and wide-eyed children hovered in the shadows, too scared to venture closer, too intrigued to go home and wait behind closed doors and drapes.

Equally curious dogs padded hopefully at uninter-ested heels. An old man settled in the rocker on the porch at the barber's shop and chewed thoughtfully on the stem of a cherrywood pipe. Been a while, he was reflecting, since a stage hit Wargrit. That, of course, had been in the good old days long back when a stage had been worth waiting on.

This outfit reaching the top end of the street there looked to be nothing special. . . .

Dust swirled under the spin of wheels and clattering beat of hoofs. Timbers groaned tiredly, tack jangled, reins tightened as Tubs Casey brought the outfit to a creaking halt at the boardwalk fronting the saloon.

Tubs set the brake and tied down the leather. Charlie Weeld gripped his Winchester.

Boden Prince, Marcus Pitch and Cornelius Tove stared from the batwings.

Nobody said a word. Nobody moved as they waited for the dust to settle.

And then the stage door creaked open.

Twenty

A gun roared from inside the stage, the blaze and kick of it rocking the unit on its suspension, spooking the team until their snorts and whinnying and Tubs Casey's shouts to them were mixed with sudden gasps, curses and groans.

Marcus Pitch crumpled where he stood, half bent to peer into the stage, his gaze wide in transfixed bewilderment, mouth lolling open, a stifled groan of disbelief and horror dying in his throat as the blood bubbled fast and thick at his gut and he finally stumbled, eyes rolling crazily, to the street.

Tove backed instantly through the batwings and disappeared into the darkness of the bar.

Boden Prince glared, snarled, thought for no more than a split second of drawing his still holstered Colt, decided against it and dived from the boardwalk to the depths of the dusty alley at the side of the saloon in what seemed to be one sudden blur of limbs and flying body.

'Sonofagoddamnbitch, what in hell's name was that?' croaked Elias Macks.

'The gambler's bought it!' yelled a man.

'Who shot him?' called another.

'Somebody in the stage.'

'The hell he did! Yuh see that – it's the drifter!'

Doc Brands swallowed as he watched the man step from the stage, pass his orders to Tubs Casey and his partner, turn for a moment and signal for Doc to join him.

'I seen everythin',' gasped Jamie Cain. 'I seen it all. Did yuh see that, Doc? Did yuh see the gambler hit the dirt? Hell, I seen it all. . . .'

'No, yuh ain't,' said Doc, heading for the saloon. 'Just keep watchin'!'

The old man in the rocker at the barber's shop bit clean through the stem of the cherrywood pipe and threw it aside in disgust.

A woman fainted. A dog licked her face.

Miras Carter scrawled in his notebook.

'Where the hell's Prince?' shouted a youth.

The town men began to gather round Macks.

Doc hurried on to where the drifter waited.

The drifting smell of cordite, stench of stale cigar smoke and liquor, old perfumes, blood and maybe death. . . . Doc sniffed and coughed as he staggered from the boardwalk to the bar, his eyes dancing wildly for a sight of the drifter, fearful that it might be Tove lurking in the shadows.

He listened to the eerie creak of the batwings behind him, blinked on the sweat in his bushy eyebrows and swallowed deeply.

'Yuh there, mister?' he hissed.

'No time now for long explanations,' said the man from the back of the bar. 'Stage passengers are safe at Doon Drift. We'll pick 'em up later. Prince's out back somewhere. Tove's mebbe with him. Can you handle things here? Keep them town men from losin' their heads?'

'Do my best,' said Doc. 'Why yuh doin' this, mister? Who are yuh?' His gaze tightened until his eyes were no more than slits. 'Can't see a damn thing in this light,' he mumbled.

'We'll talk later. Just do as I say, all right? And keep yuh heads down. Prince'll be in a mood to shoot at anythin' that moves.'

'How'd yuh manage—' began Doc, but knew in seconds he was addressing empty space. 'Yuh darn well fooled me, and that's for sure,' he murmured to himself, turning as the 'wings creaked again and Elias Macks burst into the bar.

'What do we do, Doc? Where's the man? Did yuh see that out there? Hell, how'd the fella do that? Where's Prince? Where's Tove? Where's the passengers? Yuh want for me and the boys—'

'Just hold it, Elias,' urged Doc. 'We don't want nobody runnin' wild around town right now. There's goin' to be some vicious lead flyin'. Let's try stayin' alive, eh?'

'But what if—'

The snarl of a Colt, an echoing curse, whinnying snorts of horses silenced Macks.

'Mebbe we should get that stage off the street,' said Doc stepping quickly to the 'wings. 'And watch yuh back, will yuh?'

Boden Prince slid like a snake among the jumble of crates, timbers, barrels, thrown aside flotsam at the back of the Best Bet saloon, reached a deep shadow and crouched low, wiping the back of his good hand across his sweat-soaked brow.

Where was the fellow now, he wondered, licking his cracked lips? Hell, you could never be sure; might be anywhere, do anything, same as he had when the stage pulled in.

That had taken planning, cunning, real guts. Goodbye to the Paterson girl and the fortune she would have brought as a hostage. Goodbye Marcus Pitch – sonofabitch never saw a thing till it was all too late – and goodbye Wargrit, you could bet on that, he thought, licking at his lips again. Time had come to survive, pull out while he was still breathing.

He eased carefully from the shadow, paused, listened, came fully upright, the Colt tight in his grip, and slid on towards the livery. Sure to be at least one mount there, he reckoned. Art Kinley would hardly have been fool-headed enough not to keep his own horse tucked away some place.

He slid to another shadow. Waited. A deal of activity

in the main street. Men coming, going, shouting among themselves. Somewhere to be avoided for now.

He risked a quick glance in the direction of the saloon's back door. Closed. No sign of Tove. Where the hell had he holed up! Protecting his own skin first, as ever! Still, no sign of that drifter neither. So where was he? Hidden some place. Any one of a hundred shadows, but not this one, nor the one over there, thought Prince, shifting again.

He grinned softly to himself as he made it to the shadow, the next, and on again, closing at a pace now on the corrals, stabling, barns and outbuildings of the livery. No shortage of shadows there!

But just where was the drifter?

Prince cursed quietly, cleared the sweat, took a deep breath, a fresher grip on the Colt, and slid on. Open ground to be crossed here, but no problem if he kept low, veered a mite to left and right and reached the dark side of the nearest barn without pausing.

He grunted. Time would come for Cornelius Tove when there was a reckoning to be faced. You bet! Same went for that grease-mound, Jonas Bantry. Heck, why had he let Bantry ride alone to San Apee? Should have seen all this coming. Could have figured it in one.

He moved. Fast, low, left to right. Same pace. Nothing moving save himself. No sounds save those from the street, the beat of his heart, rush of his breath.

Almost there. Take a breather in the shade. Figure on just where Kinley would stable his own mount. Then get to it, saddle up, ride out. Get the dirt and dust of

Wargrit from under his skin. He could reckon for Tove later, assuming the scumbag survived. Maybe the drifter was settling with him right now.

The side door to the barn creaked open to Prince's touch.

He blinked on the gloom, waited for his eyes to adjust to the darker surroundings. Silence. Nothing larger than a dirt bug on the move. But no sounds of a mount neither. Hell! Wrong barn. Well, no sweat. Move again, on to the next one. Take your time, no hurry, no rush.

It was the sound of a boot scuffing through straw bedding that broke the sweat in Boden Prince's neck to a trickling chill.

Elias Macks' grip on the Winchester was hot, sticky and beginning to shake. Not seeing that good either, specially not here in the barn with the shadows standing like ghosts and Boden Prince right there, only yards away. Be as easy as plugging lead to a bucket to hit the sonofabitch from here – if only he had a steady grip on the rifle, damn it!

He ran his tongue slowly over the tips of his teeth, the cracked, parched line of his lips, the sweat like a fire on his face, the anger bubbling in him as if about to burst through his skin.

Just shoot the scumbag, he told himself, his gaze wet and painful; two fast shots, no thinking it through, no doubting it, cold-blooded as Prince had been out there on the street. Just do it!

He shifted a step through the straw at his feet. A mistake! Should have stayed where he was. Prince had heard him, probably had him fixed already. Colt was in his hand too. Hell, unless he moved now. . . .

'Yuh should've stayed with the doc,' sneered Prince, levelling his aim as Macks slid clear of the deeper darkness. 'Too damned late now, fella!'

Macks heard the blaze of Colt fire, once, twice, three times, felt the heat as the Winchester spun from his grasp, a sudden rush of blood across the back of his hand, the surge of a hot-poker pain – but he was still standing, damn it, still seeing the shadows, the shapes in the barn.

'What the hell!' cursed Prince, straddling the open space now, his gun tight and anxious in his hand, his gaze wide and wild in the darkness as his eyes searched for the source of the two shots that had not left his Colt.

Macks scurried into a corner, his mind whirling, thoughts and images jumbled in mayhem, the blood dripping unchecked from his hand to the yellow straw.

'That you, driftin' man, yuh sonofabitch?' cursed Prince again. He spat noisily and backed slowly towards the deeper shadows.

'Stay right where yuh are, mister,' came the voice as if from nowhere. 'Not another step, right?'

'Who the hell are yuh? Yuh the law or somethin'? What's all this to yuh, anyhow?'

'Oh, sure, Mr Prince, I'm the law. Long time ago,' came the voice again, this time from Prince's right-hand side. 'Yuh rode with Billy Dance and his boys, didn't yuh? Sure yuh did. So yuh recall Scarcut Creek, eh?'

'That was years back,' clipped Prince.

'Not so many, not in my book, not when yuh been countin' every one of 'em since that hangin' day at Forman.'

'All that time back . . .' murmured Prince. 'I got yuh now. I know yuh, sure I do. . . . Kavanagh. John Kavanagh. Sheriff back at Forman. So how come—?'

'Yuh recall the days after Forman? Yuh got lucky and rode free, didn't yuh? Yuh remember, Prince? Bet yuh do, eh? 'Specially that homestead on the Bedrock Flat. Yuh remember that?'

'Hell, that's far back—'

'Don't lie, Prince! Yuh recall well enough. Young fella and his pretty wife.'

'Fella there pulled a piece on me, damnit. Self-defence.'

'Pulled a piece on yuh *because yuh were rapin' his wife,* f'Cris'sake! That's why yuh shot him – so's yuh could get back to his woman. Finish what yuh'd started.'

A fresh beading of sweat broke across Prince's brow, trickling like lava to his eyes. 'Hell, I don't recall that clear. She was just a woman. . . .'

'She was my sister-in-law! It was my brother yuh shot out there at Bedrock. My brother, damn yuh, and I been lookin' for you ever since. And I find you in another nest of rats – so I'm cleanin' up here, Prince, beginnin' with you.'

Elias Macks said later as how the shadows in that livery barn turned to flame and exploded in the next few seconds. 'Seemed like the earth went into a rage of noise and heat. There was blood flyin' thick as fire birds, and snarlin' and cursin' such as yuh ain't never heard. I don't figure for that fella Kavanagh knowin' when to stop the shootin'. It just went on and on and on like it would never end. . . .'

But it did, and when it was done there was just enough of the gunslinger's face still left to say as how that had once been Boden Prince, late of San Apee.

Twenty-One

'Hear that, mister? Yuh should. And hear it good. I reckon yuh just saved yourself a heap of money on set-tlin' the account with yuh gunslinger! What yuh say, Mr Tove?'

Lily Hassels made no attempt to hide her smirk as she backed to the corner of her room above the saloon, her gaze tight and watchful on Cornelius Tove. She waited until the echo of the gunfire at the livery had finally faded before adding:

'My money's on the drifter. Where's yours?'

'Shut your mouth,' growled Tove moving away from the window, his fingers tapping lightly over the inset bone on the butt of his Colt.

Lily smirked again. 'Fancy butted Colt ain't goin' to count for much against the fella out there, is it?'

'I said to shut it!'

'Yeah, and I heard yuh first time. Fact, I been hearin' yuh for years, too many by my book.' Lily folded her arms dramatically. 'Reckon I'm all through with the hearin' bit. Time we split, called it a day, beginnin' right now.'

'Sure,' drawled Tove, 'yuh do that. . . . But let me tell yuh somethin': yuh still ain't doin' nothin' 'ceptin' on my say-so. That clear? Don't be fooled none by what's happened here today. It ain't done yet.'

'Oh?' said Lily, a frown replacing the smirk. 'Yuh reckon all this no problem, eh? Yuh just lost Pitch, probably Prince, and yuh ain't seen nothin' of Bantry. So tell me, how ain't it "done yet"? Yuh got another hired gun up yuh sleeve? Not in Wargrit, yuh ain't. Fact, I wouldn't be surprised if the drifter ain't headin' this way right now. He'll have figured where you're holed-up. Take a look. See for y'self.'

Tove smiled but made no attempt to step closer to the window. 'Mebbe the fella is at that. But it don't matter none, does it? Not a mite – not while I got you along of me. When we make a move, we do it together. You take my meanin'?'

'Yuh goin' to stand back of me like yuh usually do. I'm the shield, hostage, a barrel in my spine while yuh walk out of here and figure for ridin' free. That it?'

'Close,' grinned Tove.

Lily shrugged. 'No choice, is there? You're the one with the gun. But I wouldn't give much for your future once them stage passengers marooned out at Doon Drift get to hearin' of yuh. Time they've joined up with the town folk here it's goin' to seem like yuh got half the territory houndin' yuh butt. So where we runnin' to this time? Yuh got some place planned?'

143

'*I* got some place planned. Remains to be seen who's with me.'

Lily's eyes had narrowed on the scheming glint in Tove's eyes when the sound of raised voices in the street below drew both their attentions.

'Tove?' came the shout. 'We know you're up there. Know yuh got Lily along of yuh. Well, yuh can forget any notion yuh cradlin' about ridin' outa here. Boden Prince is dead. Yuh hear that? Dead. And there's a fella here wants a word with yuh about the shootin' of McLey and Joe Blossom. Yuh'd best come down quiet, eh?'

'Well, now,' smirked Lily again, but fell back to the wall at the sudden roar and blaze of Tove's Colt, the shattering glass at the window, the tinkling shards as they scattered across the floor.

'Go to hell!' yelled Tove. 'I'm comin' out when I'm good and ready, Lily right in front of me. Yuh raise so much as a spit, and she dies. And I ain't kiddin'.'

Lily Hassels knew for certain he was definitely not kidding.

'We got the place cleared,' said a man in the gathering surrounding Doc Brands on the boardwalk fronting the saloon. 'Ain't a living soul in there save Tove and Lily. Yuh want for us to try the back way?'

'Too noisy. Too dangerous,' murmured Doc. 'Tove ain't for foolin'. Nothin' to lose, has he? He'll kill Lily soon as look at her.'

'I say we wait,' said an old-timer. 'See how the drifter

144

reads it. Damn it, this is his show. We don't want to foul up now, do we?'

'Tove's goin' to have to move before it's full dark,' said a man lounging at the 'wings. 'Close on dusk now. Another coupla hours. . . .'

'Mebbe it's the night he's waitin' on,' hissed a youth.

'Day, night, don't matter none. When he steps outa there with Lily—'

'Drifter's headin' this way now.'

Tove loosed another blaze of lead through the shattered window of Lily's room.

'He carries on like that,' muttered the old-timer ducking for cover, 'they'll be fallin' through the holes!'

Lily winced, shivered, screwed her eyes against the blast of gunfire and pressed herself tight to the wall.

'Time to show 'em who's callin' the shots round here,' sneered Tove, the sweat beginning to bead on his face.

'Why don't yuh leave it while yuh still in with a chance?' said Lily, her eyes wide and glassy. 'Damn it, yuh lost out on yuh plan to take the girl from the stage; yuh lost Pitch, Bantry, yuh hired gunman. What the hell's left worth fightin' over? Take a gamble now and yuh might just get clear. Stay here shootin' it out 'til the lead runs dry, and what yuh got? Prospect of a coffin, and not a deal more.'

'I'll do the decidin' round here.'

'Ain't makin' much of a job of it so far! And I'll tell yuh somethin' else yuh ain't thought of – yuh ain't got a horse, have yuh? How yuh goin' to ride outa Wargrit. . . ?'

'I'd figure for your life raisin' me a mount,' clipped Tove moving to the side of the shattered window. 'Lily Hassels' life for a horse? I reckon the town'd pay up to that.'

'Well, thanks!' flared Lily, pushing herself away from the wall. 'Nice to know I got some value round here. If I'd known way back, I could have sorted me a whole new—'

'Enough!' growled Tove. 'We're all through with the talkin'. We're movin'. And just so's yuh ain't under any illusions, understand this: them sonsofbitches out there don't get to playin' this out exactly to my rules and you're dead, Lily Hassels, dead as the dirt you'll be lyin' in. Yuh got that? I make m'self perfectly clear?'

Lily shivered again in the gathering gloom and chill of the room. 'Perfectly,' she murmured, staring deep into Tove's eyes where it seemed the night had already gathered.

'Now move!'

'Where's he now?' whispered Elias Macks to Doc Brands and Jamie Cain where they hugged the shadows at the side of the batwings. 'He shifted any? He still got Lily?'

'No change,' murmured Doc. 'Still at the head of the stairway. Door to Lil's room open at his back. He ain't for movin' yet.'

'We goin' to sit it out, or do somethin'? Art Kinley's

got his own mount all saddled up and ready. What yuh reckon?' Macks squinted into the depths of the deserted bar beyond the 'wings.

'The drifter – Mr Kavanagh, that is – says as how to wait,' said Jamie, licking his lips.

'Wait for what?' asked Macks. 'Hell, that scumbag's got Lily there. She must be scared near out of her skin.' He eased back to the shadows. 'Where's Kavanagh now?'

'Somewhere in the bar,' said Doc.

'Tove know that?'

'I doubt it.'

'So yuh figure for him takin' Tove when he's good and ready?' said Macks.

'Just that,' said Doc. 'When he's good and ready. Not before.'

Macks twitched his shoulders and grunted. 'Can't argue with the way he took out Prince. Hell, yuh should've seen—'

'Doc,' shouted Tove from the depths of the saloon. 'Yuh there?'

'I'm here,' called Doc.

'Gettin' awful tired of this waitin'. Now seein' as you're about the only one hereabouts worth trusting, I'm tellin' yuh to get movin'. I want a horse, back of the bar, saddled and ready to ride. Shan't ask again. Yuh got fifteen minutes – then I start shootin', pickin' off the interestin' bits of Lily here that ain't goin'to make her worth the spittin' over, time I've finished. So what'll it be? I get the horse?'

147

Doc waited a moment, swallowed, stared at Macks, Jamie, the town men gathered in the thickening evening gloom, their faces intent behind the soft glow of a single lantern.

'I'm waitin' for yuh, Doc,' shouted Tove again. 'What's it goin' to be?'

'You win,' answered Doc. 'We'll get the horse. You just make sure yuh don't harm Lily.'

'And somethin' else,' said Tove, the tone of his voice a shade lighter, more relaxed. 'You tell that driftin' fella to lay back, yuh hear? I don't want no trouble from him. He'll know what to expect if he interferes.'

'I hear yuh.'

'What the hell, Doc,' hissed Macks. 'We goin' to let the scumbag ride out?'

' 'Course we ain't,' said Doc. 'But we ain't for seein' Lily suffer neither.'

'And what about Kavanagh? When's he goin' to make a move? All very well him skulkin' round in there, but it's time—'

'Doc!' came a cracked, urgent voice from somewhere beyond the lantern glow. 'Hey, Doc!'

'He's over here,' snapped the old-timer. 'And keep yuh voice down, f'Cris'sake. We got urgent business waitin' on us.'

'Urgent business back of me too,' came the voice again. 'Bantry's gotten free, helped himself from Doc's wardrobe and is on the loose – carryin' a shooter!'

'Hell!' cursed Doc. 'Where's he now?'

'Last seen headin' to the back of the saloon here.

148

Mebbe he's for gettin' to Tove.'

'Mebbe he already has,' groaned Macks, as the men on the boardwalk watched a sudden surge of flame flash like a viper's tongue across the night-bruised sky.

'He's torched the bar!' croaked the old-timer.

'Somebody look to Lily!' yelled Macks.

But by then his words and Lily Hassels' screams were lost in the roar and blaze of Tove's wild gunfire.

Twenty-Two

It had taken Jonas Bantry some hours of patient struggling to free himself of the ropes at his wrists and ankles and finally fathom his way out of Doc Brands' loft.

It had taken only minutes to find some clothes that fitted, raid Doc's rolltop desk for the spare Colt he had always had buried back of a drawer against rowdy patients, and sidle away in the night like a bad tempered cat.

Bantry had only one thing in mind as he made his way to the back of the Best Bet saloon. He had no mind for the fates of Boden Prince and Marcus Pitch; he could not give a damn for the drifter, and felt much the same for the rest of the town, Lily included. But he sure as hell had a deep-seated longing to see Cornelius Tove pay a high price for messing up on the stage heist.

The shooting of Sheriff McLey and Joe Blossom had been one thing, but this – this whole fouled-up mess with nothing to see for it save the long shadow of the gallows some place – was not for swallowing.

Nossir! Tove would have to pay. With his life.

'I know you're in there, Tove,' bellowed Bantry above the cracking lick and spit of flame as the fire took hold among the flotsam at the rear of the saloon. 'Yuh there, sure enough. And that's where you're goin' to fry! Yuh hear me? Too late now. Fire's got a real hold here. Yuh just ain't goin' no place, are yuh?'

Bantry's face gleamed in the dancing blaze. 'Yuh should've listened, yuh know that? Should've paid heed to the warning about that drifter. Should've heard me out when I was tryin' to tell yuh. But, oh, no, yuh had to go yuh own way, didn't yuh? Same as yuh've always done. Probably figurin' on finishin' with me and Pitch, anyhow, once yuh'd got yuh hands on Paterson's money. That right? That about the size of it? I'll just bet it was! Well, I don't give a damn right now. You just fry there. Me, I'm goin' to go get m'self a horse and ride outa this two-bit hole of a town while I got the chance. And I shan't be back!'

'Somebody get to the livery, fast!' ordered Doc. 'Don't let Bantry anywhere near Art's horse. Do whatever's necessary to stop him.' He swung round to the wide-eyed youth. 'Jamie, you roust up the rest of the town folk best yuh can and get to fightin' that fire. It gets a hold and there'll be nothin' left.'

'On my way!' shouted Jamie disappearing into the shadowed street.

'Where in hell's Kavanagh?' coughed Macks, wiping the billowing smoke from his eyes.

'Forget him,' groaned Doc. 'He can look to himself. Let's get to Lily.'

'No chance,' yelled Macks. 'Tove's goin' to come outa there lead blazin'. Yuh'll be cut down before yuh can blink.'

'Damnit, we gotta try!'

'Fire's goin' to drive him out any minute, ain't it?' chipped the old-timer. 'Mebbe we should cover front and back. Be ready wherever he bolts from.'

There was a crash of timber from somewhere deep in the bar.

'I'll be back,' said Macks, and swung away to the shadows.

'Goddamnit, I ain't seen nothin' like it in my life!' grunted the old-timer. 'Gettin' a whole lot too old for it now. What yuh want from me, Doc? Want for me to go get that huntin' gun of mine? Blow a fella clean apart at ten paces!'

'Get to helpin' fight the fire,' spluttered Doc. 'Any of us come out of this in one piece, it'd be nice to think we still got some sorta town to wake to. . . .'

'Damn the hide of that fool-head storekeeper!' croaked Tove, swinging clear of a pall of smoke, the wisps of it stinging deep behind his eyes. 'I get my hands on him—'

'No time for that,' winced Lily, staggering back from the stairway to her room with its broken window and draught of night air.

'You stay where I can see yuh,' snapped Tove.

'Damnit, yuh ain't still figurin' on gettin' clear, are yuh?'

'There's still a horse out the livery.'

'Yeah, and about as much chance of reachin' it as jumpin' on the moon! Forget it. Best we can hope for is stayin' alive and gettin' outa here before the place is a ragin' inferno.' Lily choked on a sudden twist of black smoke. 'Stairs to the bar are still clear.'

'And guns waitin' at the 'wings,' sneered Tove.

'I'll take my chance.'

Tove gestured with the Colt grim in his hand. 'Yuh'll stay right where yuh are 'til I say other.'

'There ain't the time! Another five minutes and this place'll be. . . .' There was a creak on the stairs, the soft shuffle of a careful step. 'Oh, my God,' moaned Lily, and backed into the room.

Tove turned at the sound, his face wet with sweat, the sideburns curled and gleaming, his wound suddenly throbbing, the Colt probing.

'That you, Doc?' he asked, his voice dry and splintered. 'Macks? Yuh got that horse out front? I don't want no messin' here. Yuh can have the woman. She ain't come to no harm yet. All I need is that horse.'

He shuddered at a swish of flame, the mournful creak of a weakening timber. 'Let's get it done with, shall we? Yuh can have the damn town for what it's worth. And if I see Bantry on my way out—'

The two shots flashed through the smoke and shadows, the flickering swirls of flame, like blades of lightning from some ghost-lit sky. Tove's mouth dropped

153

open as his Colt slid from his grip; his eyes widened, bulged, and for a moment seemed to stare as if in some deep trance in which he saw the gateway into Hell and the faces of those waiting there.

It was a long half-minute before he toppled into the smoke-filled bar and did not move.

Lily coughed, spluttered, sweated and felt her blood run cold at the same time as she staggered out of the line of fire and palls of smoke on the stairway into the gloom of her room.

She had no doubt whose finger had been on the trigger to loose the shot that had spun Tove to the floor of the bar and settled him for dead. But where was the drifter now? Damn it, he had taken out Pitch, stood to a showdown with Prince, now Tove. . . . Had he turned on his heel and disappeared to the night in search of Bantry?

She coughed and choked on the drifting smoke. She could feel the heat of the flames, hear the crack and hiss of burning timbers. Hell, supposing she was trapped up here. Supposing the stairs were already alight and the only way out. . . .

She swung round to the shattered window. Nothing else for it, she decided, grabbing the stool from her dressing-table and swinging it with all the force she could muster to knock out the remaining shards of glass from the frame.

'Damn the sight, smells and sounds of this two-bit town!' she cursed, swinging the stool through another arc and watching the glass scatter to the street below. 'I ever get m'self out of this,' she heaved, hissed and sweated, 'and I swear, to God I'll never set foot in the place again!'

More glass shattered. The smoke thickened. Flames licked and reached across the stairs and onto the landing like tongues.

Men in the street below were shouting.

'Lily – f'Cris'sake jump, will yuh? Jump!'

'Whole place is goin' up, gal!'

'Tove's dead! Get y'self clear, Lily!'

'Just do like we say – jump!'

Lily threw aside the stool and moved closer to the hole in the wall that had once been a window. Not too bad a drop, she thought. She might get lucky. Maybe somebody would break her fall. Who cared? Another ten minutes here and she would be frying.

'Jump, Lily!'

'Don't think about it, gal. Do it!'

Lily had taken a deeper breath, glanced fearfully over her shoulder at the raging flames already hissing and spitting their way to her door, and braced herself for the leap to the street, when the thudding pound of hoofs from the direction of the livery sent a trembling shiver through her body.

'Bantry's gotten himself a horse!' came the echoing shout across the night.

'He's gettin' clear!'

A Winchester snapped and snarled into life, but the pounding hoofs came on.

'He's taken Art Kinley's mount.'

Another crack of rifle fire. The horse snorted, raced closer.

'Ain't nobody goin' to stop him!'

Damn it, Jonas Bantry, fumed Lily, you are as guilty as the rest of the rats; went along with the McLey killing, murder of Joe Blossom, and you sure as hell would have been there with your greedy hands for whatever the taking of the stage and holding of the Paterson girl hostage might have yielded.

'And another thing, yuh owe me – like hell yuh do!' she shouted, reaching for whatever came to hand and hurling it in her temper through the gaping hole.

'Take that, yuh scum!' she screamed. 'And that! And that!'

It was not until the tears were coursing down Lily's cheeks, the breath shuddering through her breasts, that her fingers settled on the bottle of medicine Doc Brands had prescribed for her.

'Aw, what the hell!' she groaned and threw the bottle to the street, almost directly into the path of the racing, flashing-eyed mount.

The explosion that followed as the bottle shattered lifted the mount high on its hind legs, tossing Bantry to a squirming heap in the street dirt.

And then Lily jumped.

Twenty-Three

'Heck, Doc, just what did yuh put in that potion yuh mixed for me? Two sips of that and I reckon I could've blasted my way clean through the Crowfoots!'

'Yes, well now . . .' huffed Doc Brands, clearing his throat importantly before crossing to the window of his parlour, 'I guess yuh might say it proved a mite potent. But, like I said, them Comanche sure as hell knew how to take care of themselves. No half measures for them.'

'Yuh can say that again,' smiled Lily ahead of a wince, as she eased her heavily strapped ankle to a more comfortable position on the couch.

'Even so,' shrugged Doc, peering self-consciously over the rims of his spectacles, 'I suppose it was kinda lucky yuh never got to takin' it.'

'And *that* you most certainly can say again!'

'Did for Jonas Bantry though, didn't it?' winked Doc. 'Hell, did it just! Never seen a fella unseated faster. Horse's fine, o'course. But Jonas, he's sittin' there in the town jail still tryin' to figure what hit him. Miras

157

Carter's told him it was the wrath of God. And mebbe it was at that, eh, Lily?'

Lily smiled again and lay back. 'Mebbe,' she murmured. 'Just glad it's all over. Sprained ankle here ain't much to complain of, is it?'

'And that'll be good as new in a week or so.'

'Sure it will, and I'm grateful to yuh for lookin' to me and lettin' me stay here, Doc. But, hell, when yuh get to reckonin' on what all this has cost; the deaths, the pain, loss, the agony of it – damn it, that takes some swallowin', don't it?' She sighed. 'I ain't suffered nothin' alongside some.'

'Enough,' said Doc, linking his hands behind his back. 'We all have, but there's t'morrow. Always a new day and always the future.'

'Yuh believe that, Doc?' sighed Lily again.

'Sure, I do, 'specially at my age! Still, yuh reckon it. . . .' He turned, and began ticking off the points on his fingers. 'One, we cleaned up the town, got rid of Tove and his rats. Bantry'll stand trial at San Apee. Two, we got ourselves a new sheriff, and I for one reckon Elias Macks will serve us well. We're goin' to rebuild the roomin'-house and repair the saloon. Some Paterson money from the bank comin' our way in thanks for what we did. Damage is bad, but given time and effort and we'll have it good as new and a whole sight more wholesome under your direction. When yuh get to it o'course.'

'Well, I don't know about that,' began Lily.

'I do, same as the rest of the town folk do. You're

goin' to stay, Lily, because we want yuh to stay. There's a life here, a future, and you're goin' to help build it.' Doc paused a moment. 'And there's another good reason,' he added carefully.

'Oh,' said Lily, 'and what's that?'

'There's Kavanagh, the drifter. He's comin' back. Said as much, just as soon as he's cleared up a few matters out Forman way. Reckons he's earned himself a decent retirement and figures Wargrit's just about the place for it.' Doc smiled. 'My guess is, Mr Kavanagh'll really be lookin' forward to seein' yuh on yuh feet again. Taken a shine to yuh, Lily, and he's got one helluva story to tell. Yuh should hear it.' He cleared his throat on a watchful pause. 'Sends his apologies, though, for not gettin' to yuh sooner at the saloon. Yuh'd jumped before he got through the flames.'

'Apologies accepted,' smiled Lily. 'Fella say when he'd be back? He give a date?'

'Not specific,' said Doc, turning back to the window, 'but I'd reckon soon after the snows. And judgin' by them clouds up there, I'd say there's a fall due any time.'

Lily pondered a moment. 'Know somethin', Doc, I think I might just stay on, at least 'til I'm up and about again and feelin' stronger.' She frowned thoughtfully. 'But tell me, just who was that fella rode in off the dirt trail, anyhow? He weren't never just plain John Kavanagh, was he, some two-bit, no-hope drifter down on his luck? Not the way he sat that horse and handled that Colt. So who was he?'

Doc turned slowly, waited a moment, and smiled gently. 'Everythin' we could all have been, I guess – given the courage.'

Lily did not answer. She was too enthralled watching the first drift of snowflakes across the parlour window.